A WERE
RIVER

An original  novel

WOLF IN DALE

CALEB ROEHRIG

SCHOLASTIC INC.

Copyright © 2020 by Archie Comic Publications, Inc.

All rights reserved. Published by Scholastic Inc., *Publishers since 1920*. SCHOLASTIC and associated logos are trademarks and/or registered trademarks of Scholastic Inc.

The publisher does not have any control over and does not assume any responsibility for author or third-party websites or their content.

No part of this publication may be reproduced, stored in a retrieval system, or transmitted in any form or by any means, electronic, mechanical, photocopying, recording, or otherwise, without written permission of the publisher. For information regarding permission, write to Scholastic Inc., Attention: Permissions Department, 557 Broadway, New York, NY 10012.

This book is a work of fiction. Names, characters, places, and incidents are either the product of the author's imagination or are used fictitiously, and any resemblance to actual persons, living or dead, business establishments, events, or locales is entirely coincidental.

ISBN 978-1-338-56912-4

10 9 8 7 6 5 4 3 2 1   20 21 22 23 24

Printed in the U.S.A.   23

First printing 2020

Interior art by Matt Griffin

Book design by Heather Daugherty

FOR BRENDAN, DYLAN, AND DREW.
(AND CONEY, TOO!)

—C. R.

PART ONE:
IN SHEEP'S CLOTHING

ONE

AS FAR AS DILTON DOILEY was concerned, if he was going to die tonight, then a graveyard was as good a place to do it as any other. It was after eleven already, and the streets of Riverdale were swamped in a velvet-thick fog that blotted out the full moon. His breath hitched, and he hugged himself a little tighter, wishing someone could save him from the awful choice he had to make . . . but he was utterly alone.

Dilton had two bleak options before him: stick to the less creepy sidewalks for the much longer and more roundabout way back home, or take a shortcut through the darkness of the old cemetery and make it there before curfew. He prided himself on not being a superstitious person, so he was glad there was no one else present to witness his embarrassing moment of indecision.

"This is ridiculous," Dilton huffed to himself, staring at

the cemetery's bent and rusted gate, annoyed by his own attack of nerves. "Get a grip, Doiley! There's nothing scary about a graveyard." Hearing the words out loud was supposed to comfort him, but the way his voice shook wasn't terribly inspiring. "It's basically a park. Nothing in there can hurt you. But if you aren't home in ten minutes, you *will* be dead."

Swallowing hard, Dilton grabbed the gate and forced it open, a high-pitched squeal from one of the aging hinges sending an icy finger up his spine. With an apprehensive breath, he took one last look around, streetlamps pouring dim, golden light into the dense mist that rolled through this stretch of town. There wasn't a soul in sight—which, frankly, should also have been comforting. Instead, it was somehow only more unnerving. *Stupid Reggie.* This was all his fault.

The Riverdale High Astronomy Club—of which Dilton was the president—met once a week after school and organized the occasional outing or special event for its members. For instance, two months ago they'd visited the observatory in nearby Midville, and ever since then the group's plans for tonight had been all they could talk about. A spectacular meteor shower had been predicted, coinciding with the first night of the full moon, and the thought of what their telescopes might reveal had been so thrilling it had almost driven Dilton to try his hand at poetry. *Almost.*

And then the weather reports had started getting worse and worse—storm systems and cloud cover, and finally this dreadful fog, and, in anguish, Dilton had at last been forced to concede that the club would see nothing—that this once-in-a-lifetime event would pass them all by, hidden behind a thick screen of vapor.

Somewhere up there right now, past the impenetrable heaviness of the fog, stars were dancing across the vault of the night sky. Meanwhile, down here, Dilton was about to go prowling between the headstones of a musty, shadowy graveyard, because Reggie Mantle—who'd joined Astronomy Club only because he wanted to beef up the extracurriculars on his college applications—had refused to trust the forecasts. He'd insisted that the group go ahead with the meeting anyway. And Dilton, because he was the president and had a duty to attend every official outing, had been forced to stay out late for the most pointless evening in history.

"It's just a park," he reminded himself nervously as the gate clanged shut behind him and he walked farther away from the gilded glow of the streetlights. "A park with hills and grass and . . . corpses."

His fingers shook as he activated his cell phone's flashlight function, nearly dropping the device into the wet grass at his feet. The mist was so thick that in less than a minute he had completely lost sight of the street behind him, the cemetery path sloping down a gentle hillside as the first crumbling headstones reared into view. Dilton shook out the tension in his shoulders, trying to clear his head. Being afraid of a cemetery was stupid; he was a man of science, and he naturally rejected the preposterous notion of anything as silly as ghosts or zombies. There was simply no good reason to view this patch of grass as any scarier or more dangerous than the sidewalk.

Even so, he muttered reassuring facts and figures under his breath as he hurried ahead, moving faster than was probably smart, ducking the wing of a gloomy granite angel that materialized suddenly in the shifting mists. He lived in one of the safest cities in the country, he reminded himself. Violent crime was at an all-time low. Statistically speaking, a person was actually more likely to die falling out of bed than they were to even be *mugged* in Riverdale.

All of these facts were true, and yet his heart still beat like a riveter's hammer when he heard an owl hooting in the gloom, the flying predator's cry eerie and mournful among the weathered graves. Licking his lips, Dilton held his phone higher and walked even faster, his shoes sliding hazardously over the moistened earth. He'd taken this shortcut before. There was nothing to be afraid of. *"The only thing we have to fear is fear itself,"* Franklin D. Roosevelt had once said. That's all superstition amounted to—nonsense that only appeared to have a basis in reality, because your fear gave it power. That owl was probably the most dangerous thing in this cemetery.

Probably.

Swallowing hard, Dilton rifled his brain for more comforting statistics, this time about animal attacks. There hadn't been a fatal one inside the city limits in at least a century. *Then again,* he thought to himself, *maybe that's exactly what the last unlucky victim was thinking to himself a hundred years ago.* But it was only the previous month that a group of campers about twenty miles outside of town were set upon and slaughtered in the night by what authorities had described as "probably a pack of dogs or wolves."

Dilton shivered in reflexive horror just thinking about it. As far as he knew, wolves weren't endemic to the area. He wasn't sure he'd ever heard of so much as a sighting of one. But surely the sheriff's department would have based this conclusion on some sort of corroborating evidence—paw prints or shed hairs at the scene, bite marks and condition of the bodies . . . It must have been gruesome. *But it had happened well outside of town.*

The light from his phone cast a shimmering halo around him, the dirt trail narrow and slick where it made another descent, and he almost lost his footing again. The fog was cold and clingy against his skin, and when he tumbled into a time-blackened headstone that had tilted off its axis, leaning into the path, he let out a yelp of fright that was swallowed by the close, damp air.

He was still breathing hard a moment later when his cry was unexpectedly answered.

From somewhere not too far off, a high, hollow note rose in the darkness, threading through the tombstones and stealing all the oxygen out of the atmosphere. There was another predator calling out in the lonely, abandoned graveyard that night . . . and this one was much bigger than an owl.

It couldn't be what it sounded like—it *shouldn't* be; the statistics were all against it. But as the bone-chilling howl soared, dipped, and then silenced, every hair on Dilton's body stood up straight. *It was a wolf.*

"Don't panic, Dilton," he whimpered to himself, nearly choking on his own tongue as he backed away between the graves, an icy band of moisture forming at his temples. "When you panic, your brain stops functioning, and you really need your brain to function right now!"

His shoulder bumped into something hard and unforgiving—a statue, materializing from the swimming shadows—and he let out another yelp. The sound of it was like a door slamming in the still, vacant cemetery, and this time sweat rolled freely down the length of Dilton's back. His chest was constricting, and his eyes frantically raked the fog.

Had the wolf heard him? How close was it? He tried to recall more statistics about how wolves hunted and whether they were scared of humans, but nothing came up. He was already panicking. And recognizing that he was panicking only made him panic more.

Spinning on his heel, he broke into a run, all of his thoughts scattering like roaches from the light. He tripped over a child's headstone, barely missed colliding with a bench, and made it about ten feet before another statue jumped out of the darkness and he slammed straight into it. Stars exploded behind his eyes, his cell phone flying loose as he tumbled to the ground, and for a nauseating moment, the graveyard spun.

He was just pushing himself up when he heard a nearby sound—the thump of something landing on soft earth, the crush of fallen leaves underfoot—and his breath caught fast in his throat. His glasses were cracked, the world a strange, schismatic blur of black fog barely kissed by the moon . . . but two bilious yellow lights gleamed in the dark before him, maybe ten yards away, the new sound of heavy, wet breaths rubbing hideously against the night.

Dilton's vision sparkled, his fear cresting as the thick muzzle and pointed ears of a canine formed around the two impossibly glowing eyes. It was a miracle that he didn't pee his pants.

This was no ordinary wolf. Aside from its brilliant, burning glare, the creature was massive, its shoulders rippling with muscle beneath a charcoal-and-silver pelt—its paws almost as big as human hands where they flattened the damp grass. The animal snapped its jaws, a string of drool spilling between yellowed fangs that had to be at least three inches long.

"No no no, *please no!*" Dilton's voice rose an octave as he scrambled backward over mud, leaves, and loose stones, adrenaline pumping through him until his blood hurt with it. His brain emptied itself completely as he lurched to his feet, wheeled around, and sprinted into the darkness, leaving the path behind.

He had no idea where he was anymore, or where he even thought he was going. There was no way he could outrun a wolf—certainly not one of that size. But he just moved faster, colliding with tree stumps and headstones, tripping over roots and divots in the uneven ground. He was sobbing so hard he couldn't have seen clearly even if the cemetery weren't choked with a stew of mist and slithering shadows. At every turn, with every footfall, he expected to feel paws slamming between his shoulder blades, monstrous teeth sinking into the back of his neck.

When he staggered past a decaying monument and slammed into a wall of granite blocks, he was sure his time was up, but somehow the wolf hadn't caught him yet, and as he stumbled his way along the stone facing, he came to a carved pillar that marked a corner. Limping around it, he discovered that he had run right into a mausoleum—stark and imposing, its partly open wooden doors guarded by an iron grate, the plinth above the entrance engraved in huge block letters: JONES.

He'd never seen it before and had no clue what part of the graveyard he was in now. The wolf was surely playing with him, letting him get just far enough ahead to keep things interesting, but long before he could ever find his way out of the cemetery he'd be cut down—*eaten*, like those campers. Statistics wouldn't save him now.

But if he couldn't *outrun* the wolf, maybe he could hide.

The gate squealed when he threw it open and again when he yanked it shut behind him, slamming the latch in place. The doors were substantially built, and their hinges were stiff, but he managed to heave them closed as well, fumbling for a lock that wasn't there, before simply throwing his weight against the wood panels and sinking slowly to the floor with his eyes shut tight in prayer. His chest heaved with sobs, and his arm shook as he wiped a trail of snot from his upper lip . . . but he was still alive. Several inches of solid wood and iron stood between him and the beast outside now, and he could stay here all night if that's what it took. Eventually the animal would get bored—eventually it would move on and hunt for easier prey.

A laugh tickled his lungs, and Dilton Doiley let it out in spite of himself—in spite of the very close brush he'd had with death. The mausoleum was dank and pitch-black, stinking of mildew, but he didn't care. Sweat pasting his hair to his scalp, he sucked in a great big lungful of air.

And as the thundering of his heartbeat finally faded in his ears, he heard it—the sound of heavy, wet breaths filling the close darkness inside the mausoleum. *He wasn't alone.*

Dilton's eyes sprang open, his chest seizing, but there was no light to see by; the stone chamber was a black void reeking of dust and mold . . . and wet fur. A pathetic mewl of distress escaped the narrow confines of the boy's stiffened lips.

"*Diltonnnn . . .*" The voice was guttural and inhuman, the sound scraping against the granite walls—and the bilious yellow light of two glowing eyes flared to life in the depthless shadows. The air thickened with the hot, gamy stench of a predator's breath, and Dilton opened his mouth to scream.

He barely even managed to make a sound before the creature lunged forward, burying its teeth in his throat.

TWO

JUGHEAD JONES LURCHED awake, his chest heaving painfully, twisted sheets wrapped like seaweed around his legs. For a long moment, he couldn't catch his breath, his heart racing as he blinked and stared in a confused daze at his surroundings. His mind was thick, an urgent memory slipping away as he gradually started to recognize the walls and windows, the posters and furniture and discarded clothes. He was in his bedroom.

Of course he was in his bedroom.

The first rays of morning light slanted across the floor, his curtains undulating with a gentle breeze coming in through the open window. Raking back the sweaty tangle of thick, dark hair that hung in his face, Jughead's fingers trembled. He'd been dreaming, he realized—that's all it was. A nightmare. The hungry, muscular kind that was so vivid it was disorienting to wake up and suddenly find yourself somewhere else.

On instinct, he checked all his limbs and appendages, sighing with relief when he found everything still attached, and then flopped back against his mattress. Already the details of the dream were fading, and he was happy to let them go. He recalled fangs and claws, blood and moonlight, tearing flesh and . . . Dilton Doiley? The bespectacled face of Riverdale High's brainiest brainiac surfaced from somewhere in the ugly quagmire of his recollections, and then vanished again. The subconscious was bizarre.

"FORSYTHE PENDLETON JONES!" His mom's voice, blasting up the stairs at a furious decibel, brought him to a heaving start for the second time that morning. "You have *three minutes* to get out that door before you're late to school, and I will *not* be calling you in tardy again!"

His body still slick with sweat, Jughead tumbled out of bed and hit the floor in a frantic heap, his hands already grabbing for the nearest clothes that seemed cleanish. Curiously, there was dirt under his fingernails—and his mouth tasted foul, like he'd forgotten to brush his teeth the night before. Gargling with mouthwash while wriggling into a pair of jeans, he shoved his arms through the sleeves of a shirt and snatched his favorite hat off the back of his desk chair. His mind was finally starting to clear as he spit a torrent of minty blue fluid into the sink—and he realized that he actually felt pretty good. For the first time in a long time, maybe even a whole month, he hadn't spent the night tossing and turning. In fact, he couldn't even remember waking up once. And, okay, yeah, he'd been trapped in a hideous dream about bloody claws and someone screaming for their life—but you win some, you lose some, right?

Minutes later, he was pounding down the stairs, his over-filled backpack slung over his shoulders. Hollering a quick good-bye to his startled mother, he raced past her and out the door, cutting a diagonal across the front lawn. The air was crisp, scented by fallen leaves and moisture just shy of turning into frost, and the chill woke him up a little more. School was twenty minutes away if he walked, and ten if he ran—and he chose a combination of the two, because the first bell would ring in seven, so he was pretty much screwed either way.

Jughead was already halfway up the block, his legs churning and his bag thumping against the small of his back, when he realized he hadn't eaten anything before leaving the house. He was usually ravenous when he first woke up—and then again after he'd been up for an hour or so, and then maybe two or three more times before lunch—but for some reason he didn't feel even particularly hungry. His steps slowed a little as he thought about it, searching for a familiar growl in his stomach that just wasn't there. A vague memory of eating something nibbled at the corner of his mind, and he frowned.

Was it possible he'd been eating in his sleep? He'd heard of stuff like that happening before, people polishing off left-overs or fixing entire meals in the middle of the night and then waking up the next day with no knowledge of it. The more he thought about it, the more he was sure he'd brushed his teeth before bed, like always, but he couldn't forget how gross and gummy his mouth had felt—even worse than on a usual morning. He squirmed a little at the idea. The notion that he might have been up in the middle of the night, doing things he wasn't aware of, was more than a little unnerving.

Plus, as much as sleeping and eating at the same time sounded gratifyingly efficient, the condition probably had serious implications, and he could absolutely imagine his mom enrolling him in some sort of intensive study for it at the university's medical school. They were always looking for volunteers to receive free treatment at the hands of beginning students, and his mom was always looking for a bargain.

Jughead shuddered all over at the very concept. He hated going to the doctor, hated even *thinking* about it. Sometimes, just the smell of antibacterial soap was enough to make him nauseous. It was called iatrophobia, he'd found out—from Dilton Doiley, in fact—and it was apparently not all that uncommon. Either way, it wasn't a fear he cared to conquer any time soon. Whatever was going on, he could wait it out and see if it fixed itself.

Skidding around a corner, he took off up the long street that bordered the old cemetery, the sun pouring early light over pavement still shiny with dew. A clean, earthy breeze sent a candy bar wrapper skittering along past his feet, but he tried not to breathe deeply—this stretch of the walk to school always gave him the creeps. Graveyards in general gave him the creeps. There were *human bodies* in there, for Pete's sake, and worms and bugs that *ate* human bodies. Again, he shuddered, his skin crawling so hard he was afraid it would beat him to his first class.

In third grade, he'd been to this cemetery on a field trip, forced by a sadistic teacher to search the headstones for the oldest and most interesting epitaphs. Jughead had spent the whole afternoon jumping at shadows, feeling like spiders were marching up his legs.

Glancing to the crest of the hillside in spite of himself, to where headstones tilted lazily out of high grass that was unnaturally lush and green—*probably because it was feeding off dead bodies*—he was hit by a sudden, disorienting wave of déjà vu. He couldn't remember the last time he'd voluntarily set foot through the cemetery's gates. (He took the longer way to school specifically because it let him avoid walking past all those creepy, age-darkened graves.) And yet . . . being here now felt like an echo. Like a moment repeated back to him from the very recent past.

He was still trying to shake off the haunting sensation a few seconds later when he reached the top of the street—and drew up short. All along the downslope ahead of him, a fleet of news vans crowded the curb, their bumpers almost kissing and their rooftops heavy with satellite dishes and antennae. Glistening yellow lengths of crime scene tape had been looped through the bars of the long-rusted gate that allowed access on this side of the graveyard, and at least four reporters stood along the iron fencing with the rich green grass behind them, speaking earnestly into their cameras.

Once again, Jughead's gaze turned back to the headstones poking out of the peaceful, rolling hills of the cemetery, to a lonely crow circling overhead, and the hangdog face of a stone angel just up the path from the gate. A sudden chill made goose bumps sprout across his shoulder blades, and he tightened his grip on the straps of his backpack. Every now and then people partied out here after dark—littered, knocked over old grave markers, or left graffiti on one of the mausoleums—but that was about the worst kind of crime this part of town had seen in ages. Certainly nothing that warranted this sort of attention from the media. It was a safe neighborhood. It was *his* neighborhood. What had happened last night?

And why couldn't he rid himself of this freaky sense of déjà vu?

Picking up speed, Jughead hurried to the far side of the street and then ran the rest of the way to school.

By the time he reached Riverdale High, Jughead was sweaty again and out of breath—and late, as usual. The parking lot was jammed with cars, but the sidewalks out front were empty of the students who always lingered as long as possible before capitulating to the first bell . . . and the flag had been lowered to half-mast. Looking at it, Jughead swallowed a growing lump in his throat.

Someone had died.

Even after he'd left the cemetery in his rearview, that vague and uneasy sense of déjà vu had clung to him. When he reached for the details, however, their edges only became softer and more slippery, just like with his dream. And it was at that moment that the first solid image from his night-mare finally surfaced: a statue of an angel, backed by fog, blood running down its face like tears—*the graveyard*. Of *course* he'd dreamed about it. He wished they didn't live so close to that bona fide ghost factory, but several generations of the Jones family were buried there, and his mom was *not* impressed by his insistence that unholy beings loose from their graves roamed the neighborhood at night, looking for souls to eat.

Hiking his backpack up higher onto his shoulders, he headed for the doors to the building. His first class of the day was chemistry with Mr. Flutesnoot, and only two minutes had passed since the final bell; as long as the man was in a good mood, and he usually was, there was a decent chance Jughead could talk his way out of being marked down as late. He was already figuring out what he'd say, going through his mental Rolodex of trusty excuses and trying to remember which ones he had used before, when he shoved his way through the main entrance and completely lost his train of thought.

The halls were packed with people. Students clustered in front of the lockers that lined the walls, speaking in low murmurs, some of them holding on to one another and crying. Everywhere Jughead looked, he saw ashen faces, somber frowns, swollen eyes. Teachers stood outside their classroom doors with helpless expressions, either making futile attempts at reminding their students that first period had started, or simply just looking on with vacant dismay—drooping inside their clothes like balloons low on helium.

His stomach turned over, and Jughead's palms filmed with a clammy sweat. Grief was so thick in the air he could practically taste it, and for some reason he couldn't understand, he wanted to turn around and escape—to run all the way back home and get into bed again. Whatever had caused this, he didn't think he wanted to know anything about it.

A large hand clapped down suddenly on his shoulder, and Jughead yipped out loud, jumping nearly a foot and almost losing his balance on the slick linoleum floor. When he turned around, he found himself staring into the wide, sympathetic eyes of his best friend, Archie Andrews. The guy's bright red hair was carelessly rumpled, his skin pale behind his freckles. "Hey, Jug. This is just . . . I can't believe it, you know?"

"H-hey." Jughead's heart was still pounding nails into the roof of his mouth, but he waved at the hallway full of stricken faces. "What happened?"

Archie blinked. "You mean you didn't hear the news?"

"I slept through my alarm," Jughead answered weakly, watching as Ethel Muggs shoved past them, darting for the girls' restroom with tears streaming down her cheeks. His stomach shrank even more. "I've kind of only been awake for a few minutes."

Letting out a weary breath, Archie shook his head, squeezing his eyes shut. "Oh, man, Jug. I don't even know how to say it—the whole thing is messed up." He took a deep breath, his expression mournful. "It's Dilton, Jug. He died last night. He was . . . he was killed in the old cemetery."

And just like that, another fragment of Jughead's dream came back with perfect clarity: Dilton Doiley, his face bloodied, his cracked glasses reflecting a pair of glowing eyes; his mouth slack in a dead man's pantomime of a terrified scream; and his torso—several yards away—with a steaming coil of bright pink innards spilling from his open stomach.

Lights flashed, Jughead's eyes rolled up, and he fell into silent darkness.

THREE

NOT A LOT OF PEOPLE understood Jughead Jones. Mostly because, quite frankly, not a lot of people tried. Then again, he wasn't exactly *asking* to be understood, either. From his crown-like hat to the jacket he almost never took off, he wanted to be seen as different, as a weirdo. If the popular kids liked something, Jughead rejected it, proudly and emphatically. Every day, he put on a show of studied indifference, governing his emotions, pretending not to care. Sometimes the whole stoic, disaffected act even fooled Archie—which is why he was not at all prepared when his best friend blacked out in the middle of the school hallway after hearing about poor Dilton.

Everyone in their crew liked Dilton, of course. Or rather, most of them did. He wasn't part of *the gang*, or whatever, but even the biggest jerks in school had trouble finding anything about Doiley to object to beyond just his general nerdery. He wasn't a "burgers after school" kind of friend, or a "come hang out at band practice" friend, but he was at least a "gives you the answer to question six" kind of friend; so it wasn't like Archie expected Jug to just . . . *not care* that the guy had been killed. But he wasn't expecting a full-on Greta Garbo swoon right in front of the whole school, either.

Archie barely managed to grab his friend before he hit the ground. "Jug? Oh crap, Jughead, are you okay?"

"*Dilton* . . ." Jughead sagged in his arms, nothing but white showing where his lids were slit open, and the name came from the back of his throat—thick, rasping, and guttural.

Archie eased the boy to the ground, propping him against the wall in a seated position. "Jug? Jughead! Can you hear me?"

The unconscious boy groaned, listing sideways, slipping out of his friend's grasp and sprawling across the tile. Archie was struggling to sit him back up again when someone knelt down beside him. Dressed in her cheerleading uniform, her blond hair pulled back in a tight ponytail, Betty Cooper took hold of Jughead's right shoulder while Archie anchored his left, and together they maneuvered him back up against the wall.

"Thanks," Archie said, giving the girl a shy smile. He never quite knew where things stood between him and

Betty. They'd all been friends since childhood, but somewhere between six and sixteen, Archie had developed rather complicated feelings for Betty Cooper. At times it felt like they were more than friends, and at other times . . . other times it felt like they knew each other almost *too* well, and that maybe it was best if they left things as they were.

"No problem." She smiled back, but there was sadness in her eyes. There was sadness in everyone's eyes today. "Jeez, I hope he's all right." With an apologetic frown, Betty hauled off and slapped Jughead across the face—hard. "Juggie, wake up!"

The boy flinched, but his eyes fluttered open, rolling back down to reveal dazed and partially focused pupils. Blinking a few times, Jughead mumbled, "Ouch. What the hell?"

"You're welcome," Betty said primly.

"You totally fainted, Jug!" Archie exclaimed, prying one of his friend's eyelids back so he could check for . . . something. He didn't actually know why you were supposed to examine someone's eyes when they'd blacked out, but he'd seen it on TV. "How do you feel? Do you need some water? Or, like . . . um. What do you give somebody who faints?"

"He needs to go to the nurse's office." Betty pressed her fingers to the pulse in Jughead's wrist and frowned. Before she could say anything, however, Jughead jerked his arm free from her grip.

"I'm fine," he croaked. "I don't want to see the nurse." Clearing his throat and dragging in some air, he added, "This isn't a big deal, I just . . . I didn't eat breakfast, and I got a little dizzy. That's all."

"You didn't eat *breakfast*?" Of all the things Archie expected his best friend to say, this hadn't even made the list. Among the few things he'd learned to count on in life were (A) gravity, (B) the consistency of getting chosen to do a math problem in front of the class on a day he hadn't done the homework, and (C) Jughead's appetite. The guy loved food. He carried snacks that he could eat between snacks, for crying out loud! "Did . . . did your house burn down?"

"Attention, students." The voice of Mr. Weatherbee, the school's principal, crackled to life through the PA system overhead. Instantly, a hush fell over the crowd filling the hallway. "Our little community here has received some terrible and shocking news today. As many of you know, Dilton Doiley—one of our best and brightest students—died last night. Out of respect for his memory, and so that the student body of Riverdale High might have some proper time to process, classes are canceled for the day. Grief counselors will be available for those who need them—"

The rest of the announcement was drowned out by the sound of people herding for the exits, respectful murmurs blossoming into excited conversations as the prospect of a reprieve from school immediately replaced their sorrow for a dead classmate most of them never spoke to anyway. Betty's expression remained troubled and unhappy, though. And regardless of his protestations, Jughead was pale, his hands trembling a little as he knotted them together around his knees.

"Come on." Making an executive decision, Archie dragged both of them to their feet. "Dr. Andrews prescribes comfort food—we're going to Pop Tate's."

👑👑👑

Terry "Pop" Tate had run the Chock'Lit Shoppe in downtown Riverdale for as long as Archie could remember—certainly his whole life, and probably longer. Probably a *lot* longer. Part diner and part old-fashioned ice-cream parlor, it was one of the few establishments in town that offered the kind of prices that the average high school student could handle, and Pop Tate himself was always happy to see even his lowest-paying clientele. It was the obvious destination for hungry kids on an unexpected day off.

Which is why Archie should have been expecting to encounter some of the people he least wanted to see when the three of them walked in. Reggie and some of his cronies—along with Veronica Lodge and a few of hers—had already beaten them there, staking out a corner booth with a view of the door, cheering loudly whenever someone entered. They were celebrating, unbothered by Dilton's awful death, and it wasn't a mood Archie wanted any part of.

The fact was, he and Reggie had a lot in common. Maybe *too much* in common, actually, because they could only seem to be friendly to each other when they weren't competing. But they were always competing over *something*. Praise, popularity, attention from girls . . . Reggie was capable of making anything into a contest. And as for Veronica? She could be thoughtful one-on-one, but Mantle really brought out the worst in her. When they were together, it was best to avoid them both.

As Archie led the way to a booth at the back of the restaurant, close to the kitchen and far away from their boisterous classmates, Betty remarked, "We're going to get an earful for not sitting with them."

"Reggie's not going to care." Shrugging off her concerns, Archie waved to Pop, whose face was shiny with sweat as he flipped patties on the cooktop. It looked like he was the only one working again. "He's surrounded by his little fan club. We'd just be a distraction."

"I wasn't talking about Reggie," Betty muttered.

As they slid into the vinyl-upholstered bench seats, Archie

hazarded a glance back at the other group and saw Veronica watching them. "You mean Ronnie? Come on—she might be a little annoyed, but she doesn't hold a grudge."

"Oh, Archie." Betty managed a wistful smile. "You sweet summer child."

Archie just blinked, a little confused. It was true his relationship with Veronica was complicated—in some of the same ways that his friendship with Betty had become complicated after they both went through puberty and everything got kind of confusing. But Ronnie was . . . Ronnie. She never stayed mad for long.

"So what can I get my favorite customers?" Pop Tate appeared beside their table, standing above them with a notepad in hand, his apron stained with chocolate sauce, grease, and ketchup. At least, Archie hoped it was just ketchup.

"I'm springing for a round of milk shakes, but I'll let Jughead order his food first while I'm deciding what to eat." Archie gestured at his friend with a wry smile, waiting for the usual back-and-forth: Jug would place a preposterous order, like three cheeseburgers with sardines and pickled beets, and Pop would throw an operatic temper tantrum about it.

But Jughead didn't even glance at the menu. His face was still ashen, and his attention was fixed on the dirt he was scraping out from under his fingernails. He mumbled, "Nothing for me, thanks. I'm not hungry."

It was another record-scratch moment—*Jughead not hungry?*—and you could have heard the proverbial pin drop. Archie and Betty exchanged a startled glance across the table, and even Pop Tate seemed to be at a loss for words. Their silence was interrupted by Reggie Mantle, though, speaking to his gathered henchmen in the corner booth at a volume usually reserved for carnival barkers. "No, seriously, you guys! He totally insisted that we have this Nerd Club meeting last night on account of the meteor shower, but we couldn't see anything because of the fog, and so everybody went home. But I said good-bye from my car while I was driving past him, so, *dude*. What if I was the last person to see Dilton alive before he got shredded by Bigfoot?"

"Why are you in Nerd Club?" Chuck Clayton asked with a snide tone.

"I don't know, Clayton, why are you on academic probation?" Reggie shot back, the retort meeting with a chorus of delighted hoots from his friends. "I'm just saying it's messed up, okay?"

"What do you mean, Bigfoot?" one of the girls asked in an uncertain way. "Someone told me it was like a drifter or something. Like some maniac hanging out in the cemetery."

"How many *drifters* come through Riverdale?" It was Reggie's turn to be snide. "And, anyway, no normal person could have ended Dilton the way they found his body,

I'm telling you." With relish, he elaborated. "The guy's head was ripped clean off his body—like, part of his spine was hanging out of his neck, and everything!"

Archie's stomach turned over, and he watched Betty's face go pale. Across the room, Veronica squirmed, muttering, "Reggie . . ."

"His guts were spilling out everywhere, one of his feet was missing, and all the meat had been stripped off his—"

"*Reggie.*" Veronica's tone was sharp enough to cut glass, and the girl who'd mentioned hearing about a drifter now had her face hidden behind shaking hands. Across from him, Archie watched Betty's fingertips turn white where they gripped the table's edge, and Jughead stared at his lap in a horrified daze.

"Come on, man, quit making stuff up," Chuck scoffed, but he sounded uneasy. "You're scaring Maria."

"I'm not making anything up." Reggie popped a French fry in his mouth, leering with satisfaction. "Am I, Ronnie?"

Everyone turned their attention to Veronica Lodge, who was nervously tearing her napkin into confetti. With an unhappy sigh, she bobbed her head. "I mean, he's being a complete ass about it, but . . . he's not making it up."

"How do *you* know?"

"Because Kevin Keller's locker is next to mine," Ronnie stated, "and Sheriff Keller was the first one on the scene when the groundskeeper called the police." That silenced the room—enough that Archie could hear Jughead swallow audibly before Veronica continued. "He basically described it just like that. Apparently it was . . . really, really bad."

"They found bite marks on the body, and 'inconclusive tracks' on the ground in the cemetery." Gleefully Reggie resumed the account. "It looks like he was chased by something—or some*one*—before they got him. The sheriff's department doesn't know if it was a man, or an animal, or both together, but get this . . ." He paused for effect. "They're calling the killer the Riverdale Ripper."

The girl called Maria started to sob, and Jughead looked like he might be on the verge of passing out again, but it was Betty who shoved herself up from the table, so quickly she knocked over the napkin dispenser. Her face white and her hands clenched into trembling fists, she stammered, "I-I'm sorry, I . . . I just . . . I have to go."

Whirling around, and slipping past a startled Pop Tate, she raced for the door and vanished into the parking lot outside.

♛♛♛

A half block from the Chock'Lit Shoppe, Betty Cooper's hands were still unsteadied by the chaotic interaction of nerves and grief . . . and dread. She struggled to make a call on her cell phone. When she finally managed the task, it rang only twice before the other party picked up.

"Well, well, well," a woman's voice drawled, low and measured—and a little sarcastic. "I was wondering when I would finally hear from you."

Betty stopped walking, shut her eyes, and drew in a breath of crisp air. She couldn't afford to sound upset. "Hello to you, too."

"I'd ask why you're calling," the woman went on, "but, then, I've seen the news."

"They're saying it was a possible animal attack."

"They always do, don't they?"

Betty could picture the woman on the other end of the call now. Most likely, she was sitting in her office beneath the massive and detailed map of the Riverdale area she had hung on her wall. Bristling with thumbtacks, it showed the locations of reported "possible animal attacks," all color coded by date to make chronological patterns easier to detect at a glance. A month ago, Betty had been standing in that office herself, helping to press a cluster of colored pins into the green area that marked a tragic campsite outside of town.

Staring into the distance, watching dark birds swoop across a pale sky, Betty said, "This time it was someone I knew."

"Well. I'm sorry for your loss."

The woman's tone was gentle, and it made Betty frown. "Stop pretending like you aren't mad at me."

"Why would I be mad at you, sweetie?" The woman's voice had smoothed into a soft, lilting purr.

"Because you told me this was going to happen!" Betty finally exclaimed, a mouse tired of being toyed with by the cat that had it cornered. "When those campers died . . . you told me it was just the beginning, and I didn't want to believe it. And now a friend of mine is dead, and it's *my fault*."

"It's not your fault," the woman relented with a heavy sigh. "This is the fault of the beast that killed Dilton Doiley— the same one that killed those poor folks in the woods last month—and no one else. Now, don't get me wrong," she hastened to add, "I'm glad you feel guilty. Guilt is a great motivator, and it'll take you a long way toward making sure you're prepared for the next time. Because, Elizabeth? You know there's going to be a next time."

"I do." Betty nodded. Freshman year, she and Dilton had been lab partners. She'd always been one of the smarter kids in class, but he was an actual genius—and yet he'd been truly humble about it, and grateful for someone who got his terrible puns. *"Hey, Betty, do you know why you can't trust atoms? Because they make up everything! Get it?"* It was a joke so bad it circled back around to being funny somehow, and her vision swam a little. "I want to be ready. I won't let this monster kill anyone else."

"Good girl." The woman's smile could be heard through the phone. "You know where I am, and you know you're welcome any time." She paused, letting significance gather before she made her next statement. "Things *are* going to get worse, Betty."

"I know," Betty returned brusquely. With another look at the sky, she added, "I'll come by after sundown. Just make sure you're ready for me."

Without waiting for a snappy comeback, she ended the call. It was true what they said: *better late than never.* But from here on out, no matter what she did, it would always be too late for Dilton Doiley, and that was something she was going to have to make peace with, somehow. If she could.

Shoving her phone back into her bag, Betty Cooper started up the street again at a determined pace, already thinking ahead about her plans for the evening.

👑👑👑

If she'd just looked back over her shoulder, she'd have seen that Archie had followed her out of the Chock'Lit Shoppe— that he'd been worried about her and had wanted to make sure she was okay. She'd have seen that he'd been standing just close enough on the sidewalk to have overheard her entire conversation, and that he was staring after her as she disappeared up the street, his brow creased in a shocked and suspicious frown.

"You told me this was going to happen." Who had Betty been speaking to? And what did she mean this was her fault? As the girl vanished from sight, a cold wind eddied around Archie's feet, and he hunched his shoulders. Whatever was going on in Riverdale, if it involved his friends, he was determined to find out the truth.

FOUR

THE SECOND ARCHIE LEFT THE table, chasing after Betty, Jughead threw his backpack over his shoulders and made a hasty exit of his own. Pop Tate called out, but the door closed on his words, a cold breeze sweeping the sound away. Slipping around the corner of the building, Jughead dashed up the street in the opposite direction of his two friends, determined to leave all conversation related to Dilton's death far behind him.

His hands trembled and his stomach cramped as he broke into a sprint, as if he could outrun the images that plagued his memory—as if he could escape the ugliness that was presently carving out permanent grooves in his mind. *"The guy's head was ripped clean off his body . . ."* *"One of his feet was missing . . ."* *"They're calling the killer the Riverdale Ripper."* That awful dream he'd had kept up with him, its horrors matching his pace step for step, refusing to let him get away.

The sound of tearing flesh and cracking bones echoed in his ears with hideous clarity; the sight of Dilton's bloodied face flashed before him—the boy's mouth yawning open in an endless, silent scream. It was enough to bring Jughead to his knees in the middle of the sidewalk, his stomach heaving as a string of dark green bile poured out between his lips.

It was just a dream. Of *course* it was just a dream. A completely terrifying, gut-wrenchingly vivid, and disturbingly coincidental one, maybe—but still, a dream. That's all it could be, and it was the only explanation he could allow himself to consider.

Unless it turned out he was having a psychotic break?

The thought made Jughead shiver. A cold sweat filmed his forehead, and he frantically scrubbed his face with the sleeve of his jacket. No, that wasn't possible—there was no history of that kind of mental illness in his family. He was being ridiculous. *It was just a dream.*

Jughead needed to get it together. His head spun as he spat foul, acrid slime onto the pavement, sucking in mouthfuls of fresh, damp air to cover the revolting taste.

Or maybe he was psychic. He'd never really believed in that kind of thing before, but it would explain everything, wouldn't it? Last night, as Dilton's final moments played out in a graveyard less than a quarter mile from his bedroom, Jughead had somehow channeled them through his subconscious mind. Right? It made sense. Sort of.

His legs were rubbery as he stood back up, his head pounding, and the world tilted and sparkled while he regained his equilibrium. The fact was, Jughead knew he definitely needed to eat something, but his stomach had been replaced by a lead weight that was almost too heavy to carry. Wiping his mouth on the back of his hand, gulping down another breath of fresh air, he started for home again—the long way, this time.

But the long way wasn't much better. To get home without passing the cemetery, Jughead was going to have to walk through the *second* creepiest part of town: the old lumber district. About a hundred years earlier, Riverdale had been one of a dozen cities in the region with a thriving lumber industry. Trees were harvested from the dense forests that climbed the endless hills, the local mills processing cedar, oak, pine, and maple, and storing the resulting timber in vast yards that anchored the west end of town. Hundreds made their livelihoods from the business of wood—thousands, if you counted the haulers and speculators, the builders who put up homes for the workers and warehouses for the entrepreneurs.

The economy had changed drastically over the past century, however, and almost all the mills had long since been closed, the structures demolished or left to rot on their foundations. Riverdale's west end was practically a ghost town these days, the lumberyards and warehouses abandoned, given over to the dominion of rats and raccoons.

Out of the ghost-filled frying pan and into the rat-infested fire.

In this neighborhood, the streets were wide and the sidewalks narrow, a purpose-built feature designed for the convenience of the truckers and flatbed drivers, whose vehicles were forced to perform a terrifying square dance every time they pulled in or out of the yards' entrances. So the chilly wind had plenty of room to build up strength as it hurtled over the pavement, shaking damaged fences of chain link, tossing garbage at Jughead's feet, and nearly blowing the hat off his head.

It was bracing, though, and felt good against his overheated face. He hated this part of town almost as much as he hated the graveyard—the raccoons could become viciously territorial when they had babies to protect, and the rats were . . . well, they were *rats*, and they were filled with actual, very gross diseases—but at least the area was quiet. For the first time since he'd arrived at school that morning, Jughead was alone with his thoughts, and he could finally stop pretending that he wasn't freaking out.

Dragging his hand along a length of fencing, the metal mesh clattering rhythmically, he told himself to be rational. If his dream had really been second sight, what did that mean? Did he have a responsibility to tell someone? In the movies, if a guy had psychic visions of a murder, it almost always got him into trouble. He'd tell people, and no one would believe him—except for the killer, naturally, who would hear about it somehow and then drop by the guy's house with an ax or a chain saw to make sure he couldn't convince anyone he wasn't nuts after all.

Or if the guy with the visions tried to ignore what he was seeing, the dreams wouldn't leave him alone. He'd just keep having them, more and more frequently, until finally one of them revealed a vital clue that would point to the killer's identity. The problem was, Jughead realized as he reached the end of the chain link—a cold, greasy lump sticking in his throat—everything he could remember from his dream he had seen *from the killer's point of view.*

And despite the scrubbing he'd given his hands over the sink after he'd woken up that morning, there were still dark half-moons of inexplicable dirt trapped under his fingernails. At least, he *hoped* it was dirt. When he held his hands up to the light, the stuff almost looked like dried blood . . .

A sudden rattling noise from behind him brought him up short, and Jughead spun around on his heel—but the street was still completely empty. Almost disquietingly so. He waited for the sound to come again, for something to happen that would reassure him it was just the wind or one of the creepy animals that made their homes in the empty ware-houses . . . but aside from the faint whistle of air cutting through the diamond lattice of chain link, he heard nothing.

It occurred to him then, finally, that the neighborhood wasn't just deserted of people; he hadn't seen a single living thing at all since he'd left the Chock'Lit Shoppe. Aside from the usual vermin, this part of town was typically crawling with stray cats that feasted on the rodents and birds that fed off the ants and other insects. But as he stood there waiting pointlessly for the noise to repeat itself, his throat bobbing up and down as that lump refused to budge, Jughead realized that the only living thing around was *him*.

The emptiness was unsettling—just one more part of this terrible day that felt all out of place—and somehow it brought a cold, clammy sweat to his neck. Suddenly, what he wanted most in the world was to be at home again, to have all of this behind him so he could maybe start the day over. Forcing that lump down his throat at last, Jughead turned back around . . . and ran right into a tall figure that stood directly in his path.

Letting out a shriek, Jughead lurched away, nearly losing his balance; when the figure started to laugh, the boy blinked hard, his heart beating so fiercely that his vision pulsed with bright veins of light. The person laughing at him was some-one he knew. "B-Bingo?"

"Oh, man, you oughta see your face!" Standing before him, where a moment ago there had been no one at all, was Jughead's cousin Bingo Wilkin. "In fact, hold on—let me get my phone and I'll take a picture."

As Jughead caught his breath, he considered—and not for the first time—how hard it was to believe that he and his cousin shared actual DNA. From his clothes to his hair to his personal life, everything seemed to come easy for Bingo. He was popular and athletic, he sang and played guitar in a band (called The Bingoes, the narcissist), and even when he screwed up, people couldn't wait to give him another chance. By contrast, Jughead had always been the Weird Kid, the gawky outcast whose language no one spoke and few had ever cared to learn. The universe was maddeningly unfair.

Still laughing, Bingo started digging into his pockets, and a scowl creased Jughead's face. Slamming a bony fist against his cousin's shoulder, he exclaimed, "What the hell is wrong with you, man? You almost gave me a heart attack!"

"Whoa, chill out, okay?" Bingo stepped back, holding out his hands like a hostage negotiator dealing with an unstable bank robber. "I'm sorry I scared you! I thought you could take a joke."

It wasn't a joke, Jughead wanted to spit back. A joke is when you say something funny in order to make people laugh; messing with somebody else in order to amuse yourself at their expense is a *prank*. A lifetime of being Riverdale's signature oddball made Jughead intimately familiar with the distinction, and he was sick of people pretending that the second one was as harmless as the first. "A friend of mine got killed last night, Bingo. I'm not exactly in a laughing mood, and jumping out of nowhere to scare me when there might be a homicidal maniac on the loose"—*"They're calling the killer the Riverdale Ripper"*—"is not freaking cool!"

"Okay, okay!" Bingo held his hands up higher, sighing theatrically and rolling his eyes. "I give up, all right? Like I said, I'm sorry I scared you—I mean it." Rolling his shoulders a little, he rubbed the back of his neck. "And, you know . . . I'm sorry about your friend, too. I heard them talking about it on the news today. Tough break, huh?"

"Yeah, it sucks," Jughead replied, jamming his own hands into his pockets and looking at the ground. Fear and confusion about Dilton's death and that awful dream still paraded around his brain, crashing their cymbals together, and he was terrified that if he looked Bingo in the eye, the guy would know exactly what was going through his head. "What are you doing in Riverdale, anyway? Don't you have school?"

Bingo lived in Midville, one town over, where crime was arguably even lower than in Riverdale—especially just now—and where there were fewer rat-infested lumberyards and haunted, murdery cemeteries to drag down property values.

"Teacher strike." Bingo gave a foxlike grin, all his teeth showing as dimples formed in his cheeks. It was the kind of expression that belonged on the face of a salesman or a con artist—and Jughead had a feeling that right now he was the mark.

"Wow, lucky you," Jughead grumbled.

"Anyway," Bingo slung an arm around Jughead's shoulders and started walking with him down the sidewalk, "most of my friends decided to go to the lake today, but it's, like, fifty degrees out, so I was all, 'Screw that.' Then I heard that school was canceled in Riverdale, too, and I figured I'd come see what my favorite cuz was up to!"

Jughead was Bingo's only cousin who lived within about a hundred miles, and the rest of the possible qualifiers for "favorite" were all five or under, but he decided not to bother pointing any of *that* out, either. "How'd you know where to find me?"

"Are you kidding? I could smell you from home." He thumped Jughead on the shoulder this time, but even though he smiled at his own joke, something strange flickered in his eyes. Then he laughed. "Just kidding—although you probably should wash your clothes more than once every six months, dude."

"Ha ha," Jughead returned in monotone, wishing they could walk a little faster.

"Actually, I figured you'd be at the Chock'Lit Shoppe with those kooky friends of yours, but I guess I just missed you." A gust of wind ruffled Bingo's hair, and he combed his fingers through it, taming it without any thought or effort. "The old guy who works there told me which way you went, and when I saw you walking all by yourself like a sad, pathetic loser, I decided to have some fun!"

"Well, mission accomplished, I guess."

"So, the million-dollar question is: What awesome, fun stuff are we gonna do on our day off?" Bingo asked, his eyes lighting up with the promise of mischief.

Jughead's heart sank. As annoying as his cousin could be, he didn't really hate the guy, but their respective ideas of "fun" rarely looked anything alike, and past experience proved that Bingo had the stronger will. If Jughead went along with him, they'd probably end up doing something dangerous and stupid—like the time they raced skateboards down an abandoned parking ramp and Jughead ended up having to get twelve stitches when he lost control and smashed into a cement post.

"I don't know, man. I've been feeling sick all day, and, like, a friend of mine just died, you know? I kinda just want to get back into bed and sleep until next year."

To his surprise, his cousin didn't immediately argue with him.

"Prediction!" Bingo announced, squeezing his eyes shut and pressing his fingertips to the crown of his head. "You will sleep for three—no, four—hours, you will wake up feeling like a million bucks, and you will be starving!" He opened his eyes again, flashing that same, sharp-toothed grin. "Lucky for you, my parents are going out tonight and will be leaving their credit card behind so their son can order as much pizza as he and his favorite cousin can scarf down."

"That sounds cool, but I don't think—"

"Save it, cuz!" Bingo actually pressed a finger against Jughead's lips to shut him up. "It's not healthy to be all sad and miserable all the time, so don't argue with me about it. You're gonna sleep this off and feel great later—and don't you kind of wanna get out of Riverdale for a while anyway? I mean, not to 'go there,' or whatever, but your buddy was killed, like, a minute from your house." With a grimace, he stuffed his hands back into his pockets. "So come hang out at mine for a while. We can finally watch that zombie apocalypse movie you never shut up about. Plus, The Bingoes cut a new demo, and I need somebody who isn't a total butt-kisser to listen to it and tell me how it is."

Bingo smiled, rocking on his heels as he waited for an answer, the wind ruffling his hair again. He expected a yes, because that's the only answer he ever got—and if he didn't get it at first, he'd just keep trying until his cousin couldn't take it anymore. The only hope Jughead had of getting home any time soon was to give in and then resume the argument later. Like, over the phone, with Bingo all the way back in Midville, where he couldn't do anything about it but be annoyed.

"Yeah, fine," Jughead said at last, and Bingo pumped his fist in a dorky celebration of victory. "I'll call you when I wake up, or whatever."

"My parents are leaving at seven thirty, so be over at eight!" Clapping Jughead on the back, Bingo started down the street with a good-bye salute. "And bring your appetite!"

Jughead watched until his cousin turned a corner and disappeared from view, until the street was empty again, and the only sound was the wind cutting through the chain-link fence. His stomach still tied in knots, he looked back down at the dark substance caught under his fingernails, and an eerie sense of certainty swept over him in that instant. Whether it was genuine ESP or just plain old paranoia, he was suddenly convinced of one thing: More death was on its way to Riverdale.

FIVE

FOR AS LONG AS ARCHIE could remember, his family had lived next door to the Coopers, and he'd had a view of Betty's bedroom window from his own. As kids, they'd played charades or performed puppet shows for each other across the divide between their homes, and as tweens, they'd exchanged secret messages at night, using flashlights to blink out strings of Morse code when they were supposed to be sleeping.

Recently, it had become a little more awkward for them to have such an intimate view of each other's personal space, and so Betty's curtains were drawn more often than they weren't. Even so, the soft glow of light through the peachy fabric that backed the panes, and the movement of a shadow in the room beyond, was enough to tell Archie that the girl was home. And when that light went suddenly dark at exactly a quarter to eight, the redheaded boy snapped to attention, crawling to his windowsill and peeking over the edge for a side view of the Coopers' front porch.

It took only a minute for Betty to appear, dressed in yoga pants and a leather jacket that he had never seen before. As she strode down the front walk, headed for the Volkswagen Beetle she drove—a car that had belonged to her sister, until Polly went away to college, where she couldn't afford to keep a vehicle on campus—Archie raced out of his room. Pounding down the stairs, bolting through the kitchen for the back door, he shouted a garbled explanation to his parents and hurried out into the night.

Betty was just pulling away from the curb, her rear lights glaring at him like bright, angry eyes as he dashed for his own car, lunged behind the wheel, and cranked the engine to life. His back was sweating as he accelerated after her, his headlights off so she wouldn't notice him right away—and he knocked over two trash bins and nearly took out a mailbox in his desperate haste to make sure she didn't get away.

"I'll come by after sundown. Just make sure you're ready for me." He'd known Betty Cooper his entire life, from coordinated Halloween costumes to uncoordinated middle school dance moves; what was she hiding from him? And what could it possibly have to do with what happened to Dilton? *"A friend of mine is dead, and it's my fault."* Wherever she was headed,

Archie had to know. If she was in trouble, there might be something he could do to help.

Or maybe . . . maybe she *was* trouble. Shaking his head, Archie tried to rid himself of the thought. It was absurd; this was Betty, for Pete's sake—there was no way she could be up to something *nefarious*. Somehow, there had to be another explanation.

He kept Betty's car in his sights but did his best to hang back as far as possible. Archie was shocked when, after a few minutes, he realized they were headed to the west end of town—the lumber district. There was nothing there but feral animals, collapsing buildings, and illicit dump sites for car parts, furniture, and electronics that people didn't want to haul the extra fifteen miles to the actual junkyard between Riverdale and Midville. Archie was trying to figure out what business Betty could possibly have in such a rundown and potentially dangerous neighborhood, when the Beetle slowed and veered into the wide, sloping driveway that serviced one of the neighborhood's aging warehouses.

Pulling swiftly to the curb, Archie killed his engine and yanked a pair of child's binoculars—the only ones he'd been able to dig up on short notice—from the pocket of his letterman's jacket. Through them, he watched Betty come to a stop before a fenced gate that stretched across the entrance to the warehouse's lot. He watched her get out of the car, use a key to undo the padlock that secured the chained barrier, and drive onto the lot. Moments later, she returned on foot and looped the chain back around the gateposts from the inside, replacing the padlock again.

Drumming his fingers on the steering wheel of his car, his face pulled into a brooding frown, Archie gave himself a pep talk. He wanted to know what was going on inside a creepy, supposedly abandoned warehouse in a creepy, supposedly abandoned part of town. The area was filled with terrifying, cat-sized rodents, and probably also a gang of mean and fashionable punks—like the ones who always populated the bad parts of town in the movies—but the only way he was going to know is if he *did it*.

Cursing Betty for doing whatever she was doing that led them here, and cursing himself for not thinking to bring a weapon when he left the house, he eased out of the car. The air was damp, soured by a lingering smell of decay, and as Archie scuttled across the street, the hairs lifted one by one along the back of his neck. Choosing a section of the fence farthest from the few lampposts they bothered to do maintenance on anymore in the lumber district, he found a toehold in the chain link, reached up with his hands, and started to climb.

To his credit, he only almost fell off twice. When he landed again on the other side of the fence and immediately lost his footing, he also just missed tumbling into a stagnant pool of dirty water that filled a pitted section of the warehouse lot's crumbling pavement. The building itself was nondescript—two stories, boxy and industrial, the color impossible to determine even with the generous illumination of the full moon. From this angle, Archie could see a pair of small square windows just below the roofline, their grimy panes lit from within.

Crouching low, he darted across the blacktop, not at all sure what he was doing. There was a heavy-looking metal door that faced this side of the lot, but the security light above it was out, and Archie had a feeling he wouldn't get a very good reception if he just knocked and politely asked to come in. Betty's car was parked nose-in against the wall to the right-hand side of the lonely entrance, and two other cars, neither of which he recognized, were parked beside it. She wasn't here alone.

He tried the handle on the door, but it was locked. From where he stood, he could hear music playing inside, and he wished there was some way he could climb up and peek in through the windows. They were at least fifteen feet up, though, and the side of the warehouse was completely flat. Inching along the perimeter, he rounded a corner and stepped into deep shadows, where the building blocked both the moon and streetlight. Here, to his surprise, he found a small, square window at shoulder height—with a badly damaged screen.

A little elbow grease was all it took to force the screen out of the frame, at which point he confronted a single-hung pane of frosted glass. It slid up maybe ten inches before it caught fast, leaving a small, rectangular hole that gave Archie a view of nothing but darkness inside. It wasn't big enough to pass a normal-sized microwave through, but if he took off his letterman's jacket and held his breath, he was pretty sure he could make it work.

Over the summer, Archie had spent a lot of time in the weight room, trying to build up the kind of physique that he hoped would catch the attention of the girls in his life. Now, however, he regretted every single overhead press and lateral raise he'd done when he stuck his head and right arm through the opening . . . and immediately stuck fast, his left shoulder unable to fit past the narrow frame. With some considerable kicking and twisting, however—and the shredding of about six inches of important skin off his very personal rib cage—he managed to force his way through at last. Tumbling headfirst through the gap, he dropped into the shadows.

The air left his lungs as he crash-landed on a hard floor next to the porcelain base of a pedestal sink. As his eyes adjusted to the gloom, Archie took in the pale, cracked underbelly of a nearby toilet, and a mop and bucket propped against the wall. He was in a bathroom, the tile beneath him dusty but otherwise not unclean. The music was louder now, something high-octane, with a throbbing beat, and he could make out a faint glow coming in under the door.

Grabbing his jacket from where he had dropped it, and easing the door open with care, Archie stepped into a dim corridor, light slanting in from the far end to cast the flaking plaster of one wall into high relief. The music was louder still—synthesized horns and a frenetic rhythm, something that belonged in a dance club—and Archie tiptoed in its direction. Along the narrow passage, doorways to either side stood open, empty sockets so filled with darkness that it was impossible to guess what secrets they guarded. But when he reached the point where the hall ended, opening abruptly onto a vast space that soared all the way to the roof, he drew up short and gaped in shock.

Right in the middle of the otherwise empty warehouse, caught in the crossfire glare of floodlights angling down from the ceiling, stood some sort of massive obstacle course. Ramps and hurdles, ropes and rings, irregular barricades and precarious, spring-mounted beams sprawled across a flooring of athletic mats. As the music thudded away, a disembodied voice filled the air from unseen speakers, shouting, "*Go!*"

Instantly, a figure raced out from the shadows on the far

side of the warehouse, charging for the obstacle course with a fierce expression. Wearing yoga pants and a loose-fitting T-shirt, her blond hair pulled back in a tight ponytail, it was Betty Cooper. Leaping into the air, she launched herself over the initial barricade headfirst, landing in a tuck and rolling to her knees. Two objects sprang from the floor on either side of her, cardboard circles, each marked with a bright red X—and in a single, deft move, so fast Archie didn't even see her draw, she produced a pistol from a hip holster and fired two shots. Capsules of black paint burst over both targets, dead center, and Betty was on her feet again.

She leaped onto a balance beam next, which wobbled and swung under her weight, the springs stretching and rebounding unpredictably. As she pranced across, more X-marked circles appeared, snapping out from behind the barricades—three that were red, and two that were orange—and Betty fired with lightning reflexes. Black paint burst across the red targets only, and the girl lunged off the end of the beam, diving into another somersault to pass beneath a padded crossbar.

She moved like a machine, swinging between dangling ropes, dodging foam projectiles that launched at her unexpectedly from floor-mounted cannons, and throwing herself over barriers while simultaneously aiming and firing with astonishing accuracy. Archie forgot himself as he watched, openmouthed, awed by the performance he was witnessing. He'd seen Betty do backflips and tumbling passes on the field with the other cheerleaders at Riverdale High; he'd always known she was an athlete. But he had no idea she was capable of something like *this*.

When she reached the end of the course, Betty's chest heaved, and her face and neck gleamed with a thin veneer of perspiration. The music ended abruptly, and Betty bent over, her hands on her knees as she tried to catch her breath.

"Adequate," came the woman's booming voice over the unseen speakers again, "but you hit two orange targets and missed a red, and you're almost four seconds over time. Take a short break, and we'll reset."

"The target colors are too similar," Betty complained, shouting irritably at the shadows that surrounded the obstacle course. "You can barely tell them apart!"

"That's the point. Sometimes you can barely tell your targets apart, Betty. Your job here is to figure out how to make that an instinct."

"I hate this," Betty muttered, her voice carrying through the otherwise empty warehouse, but there was no answer. She scooped a bottle of water off the floor and took a long drink, while Archie shifted his feet—hovering in the dense gloom that filled the corner where he'd emerged from the narrow hallway. He wanted to confront her, to ask what all this was about, and what it could possibly have to do with Dilton. But he was also starting to realize just how out of his element he was, and how it might be best to ask her about all this on more neutral turf. Like maybe at school, where there were lots of people around and she couldn't pound him into the floor.

"Excuse me, sir," came a woman's voice from immediately behind him—the same voice he'd just heard from the speakers, only now it was swimming out of the darkness at his back and making his blood run entirely cold. "Do you mind if I ask to see your invitation to this party?"

Very slowly, his hands out at his sides, Archie turned around to face the person addressing him. But he'd barely opened his mouth to defend himself when a booted foot slammed against his chest, stealing the breath from his lungs and sending him hurtling backward through the air.

👑👑👑

As much as Jughead hated to admit it, his cousin was right. The second he got home, he crawled between his sheets, where he tossed and turned—still nauseous and sweaty, plagued by the vision of Dilton's silent scream—until he finally dozed off. Then, true to Bingo's prediction, he woke again after about three hours of a deep, dreamless slumber. His thoughts fuzzy with a naptime hangover, he was surprised to find that he felt . . . almost refreshed. Not hungry, exactly, but for the first time all day he didn't feel like he was being punched in the stomach from the inside.

He still had no intention of taking Bingo up on his invitation, no matter how hard it was to imagine turning down an offer of free pizza. The things he couldn't explain, the sights and sounds that were starting to feel less and less like a dream and more and more like a memory, had him rattled all the way through. Nothing appealed to him about trying to socialize—to put on a fake smile and pretend he wasn't scared of his own brain.

But Bingo proved right a second time when Jughead wandered downstairs, finding his mother sitting in front of the television. One story after another flickered past on the screen, an endless barrage of news coverage about the grisly death and dismemberment of Riverdale High's most accomplished student only a quarter mile from their front door. Dilton's yearbook picture, atmospheric shots of the cemetery, and unsettling crime scene photos showing the boy's shattered eyeglasses and a blood-soaked scrap of fabric made up a horrific montage.

Thirty seconds later, Jughead was dialing his cousin and asking if the invitation still stood. The only thing worse than faking his way through an evening of pizza and movies would be faking his way through an evening of "Local Teen Torn to Pieces in Old Cemetery."

To his surprise, hanging out with his cousin ended up being . . . kinda fun. His aunt and uncle had a finished basement with a massive entertainment center, and the two guys sat in beanbag chairs, stuffing their faces with food while watching zombies take over the world. Bingo mocked the movie all the way through, but the minute the credits started to roll, he was nagging Jughead about watching the sequel next.

After that, they had a competition to see who could drink a two-liter of soda the fastest, and suddenly, Jughead realized that he was actually smiling. Whole hours had gone by, and he hadn't thought about his nightmares or Dilton Doiley even once. For the first time since he'd woken up that morning, he was starting to feel like his old self again, and he had his cousin to thank. He almost didn't want to admit it, but hanging out with Bingo had been exactly what he needed.

When their chugging contest was over, they finally put on the new demo that The Bingoes had cut, and Jughead gave it his undivided attention.

"Well?" Bingo asked with an anxious look once the last note played. "Let me have it, Jug—both barrels. How bad do we sound? Should I sell my guitar?"

"Gimme a break." Jughead fixed the boy with a level stare. "This track is great, and you know it. You're just fishing for compliments."

A cocky smirk pulled at Bingo's mouth. "Maybe a little. But 'great' isn't good enough, man—it has to be better than that. It has to be perfect!" He rubbed his eyes in frustration. "We've been pitching a couple of record labels, and one of them asked to hear more. This needs to clinch the deal."

"Maybe you should replace the lead singer," Jughead suggested.

"I *am* the lead singer, you dill weed."

"That's fine, we all make mistakes." Jughead tried to dodge the friendly blow Bingo aimed at his shoulder, but he wasn't quite fast enough. "Now that we have that out of the way, is there any more pizza?"

Bingo arched a brow, his expression shifting a little. He looked almost . . . sly. "We finished it all, man. Are you really still hungry? That was a lot of food."

"Uh . . . yeah, I guess I am." Jughead looked over at the pizza boxes scattered on the floor of the basement—three of them, the cardboard stained with grease. Had they really eaten that much? Because he sure didn't feel like it. In fact, his stomach even growled a little. "I must be feeling better. Can we order some more?"

"You know what?" Bingo got to his feet, stretching out

his arms. He had broader shoulders than Jughead, but the same long, wiry limbs. "I could probably keep eating, too, but I wanna go out. I'm feeling, like . . . restless, you know?"

Jughead started nodding even before Bingo was finished speaking. He hadn't been sure how to pinpoint the agitated buzz that had been growing inside of him all evening long until Bingo said the word out loud—*restless* captured it. He'd thought he was just anxious, still bothered by the day's events, but it was almost like he was itching under his skin. He stood up, following his cousin to the stairs. "Yeah, okay. Going out sounds good. Where to?"

Bingo glanced over his shoulder, his lips pulling into that wide, toothy grin of his. "Actually, I'd like it to be a surprise."

It seemed like a weird thing to say, but as long as they got food, it didn't really matter to Jughead where they went, so he just followed his cousin up the stairs and into the Wilkins' kitchen. Once there, Bingo headed straight to the back door, tossing it open and starting outside. Pausing next to the vintage gas stove—all porcelain, chrome, and white enamel—Jughead cleared his throat.

"Uh . . . aren't you forgetting something?"

"Like what?" Bingo stopped in the doorway, the full moon creating a soft, silvery halo in his auburn hair.

"Like, I don't know, *pants*?" Jughead made an up-and-down

gesture at the guy's body, clad in just shorts and a T-shirt. He didn't even have shoes on. "It's, like, forty-five degrees out."

Bingo looked into the night, a damp, chill wind shaking tree branches that scrabbled against the glass of the kitchen window, and laughed. "So what? It was even colder in the cemetery last night, and you didn't complain then."

The room tilted suddenly, Jughead's chest going tight as his heart squeezed upward. His tongue sticking to the roof of his mouth, he forced out, "W-what did you say?"

"Why?" Bingo stepped back into the kitchen, still smiling, eyes fixed on his cousin's. "What do you think I said?"

An awful, tingling silence stretched out between them as Jughead struggled to figure out an answer to the question. He couldn't have heard what he thought he heard, and he couldn't bring himself to repeat it even if he was right . . . but everything about this moment suddenly felt off and frightening. He unstuck his tongue a second time. "I think . . . I think I better go home—"

"Don't wuss out on me now, cousin." Bingo's hand shot out so fast Jughead didn't even see it move, the boy's fingers closing tight around his wrist in an iron grip. "I'm starting to get pretty hungry myself, and I don't feel like eating alone."

His other hand shot out next, his fingernails ripping the flesh of Jughead's exposed forearm—and as blood rose to the surface, a pain shot through him unlike anything he'd felt before. It stung and then sizzled, burrowing into him like a parasite and hurtling up his veins; the air squeezed from Jughead's lungs, the muscles in his arms and legs locking up, and a cramp speared his jaw. How could a simple scratch cause this much agony? *What was wrong with him?* Eyes bulging, he tugged at his cousin's grip, wheezing for air. "Help . . . can't . . . *breathe* . . ."

"Don't fight it, Jug," Bingo said soothingly, his voice muffled and distant. The light in the small kitchen began to throb, and Jughead was certain he was starting to hallucinate, because he could swear his cousin's eyes were glowing a bright yellow. "It hurts worse if you resist, so just relax and let it happen . . ."

"Let . . . w-*what* . . . *happ*—" He couldn't finish. The pain exploded inside of him, the muscles in his back cramping so hard he heard his spine crack. His legs twisted violently—the knee joints snapping the wrong way, bone bulging against skin—and horror swept through him. A guttural, inhuman roar escaped the back of Jughead's throat . . . and everything went black.

SIX

SOMETIMES, BETTY LIKED TO imagine that she lived in a parallel universe, where the Coopers were just another ordinary, small-town family leading normal lives with normal problems. In her fantasies, she grumbled about homework, maybe had a little dating drama, and she had never had to learn how to bring metal to its boiling point so she could cast her own bullets in her parents' basement.

In this parallel universe, of course, the Coopers didn't live in Riverdale. After all, the reason Betty's life was so complicated was because her great-great-great-grandfather—Elijah Henry Cooper—moved to the area back in the late 1800s. A mill worker by trade, his desire was *also* to lead a normal life; but all of that changed one fateful night in 1893 when, during an evening stroll outside town, Elijah had a terrifying encounter that would alter the course of his life . . . and set a course for generations of Coopers to come.

Almost as soon as Cooper children could walk, they were learning how to roll with a punch, how to assess a dangerous situation, how to expect the unexpected. By the time she was eight years old, Betty had memorized her great-great-great-grandfather's many journals; by the time she was ten, she was studying judo, jujitsu, and krav maga; and by the time she was twelve, she was a crack shot. The Coopers also learned a lot of handy tips for washing blood out of their clothes.

The whole point of the pop-up cardboard targets in the obstacle course, with their exasperatingly similar coloring, was to condition her to be prepared—to react without having to think first. That's why, when a redheaded figure came flying out of the shadows, crash-landing on the cement floor and slewing to a stop at her feet, she had her pistol out and pointed right at his forehead before she remembered it was only loaded with paint capsules.

And before she recognized who she was aiming at.

The boy coughed and groaned, clutching his chest, and her eyes bulged. *"Archie?"*

"Uh . . ." He blinked up at her, trying on something that looked like a smile. "H-hey, Betts."

"Let me guess." A woman's voice boomed from the shadows, almost as loud as it had been over the speaker system just moments earlier. "A friend of yours?"

Stepping out of the gloom, the floodlights gleaming on a cascade of shiny black hair and even shinier leather pants, a woman with dark brown skin and formidable muscles in her shoulders and upper arms stopped right in front of Archie. Glaring down at him like she'd just found an insect crawling along her arm, she spun a nickel-plated handgun—a real one—around her finger and then racked the slide.

"He used to be," Betty answered, her eyes narrowing into slits as she watched Archie's face turn paper white. The warehouse and everything inside it was part of an enormous secret that she had once sworn her life to protect. Only a handful of people in Riverdale had any business knowing about it, and her next-door neighbor was *not* one of them; the only way he could have ended up there was by spying on her. "If you want to kick him some more, be my guest."

"*Wait!*" Archie shouted, throwing his hands up just as the barrel of the gun leveled with his freckled nose. "I didn't see anything, I swear it, and if you let me go, I . . . I promise I won't tell anyone what's going on!"

The woman cocked her head to the side. "And just what is it that you think is going on?"

"Um." Archie looked from her to Betty and back again, and then twisted his neck to take in the obstacle course. "Is this some kind of fight club?"

"Betty . . ." the woman growled through her teeth.

"Archie, just what the hell are you doing here?" Betty grabbed him by the shirtfront, hauling him into a sitting position so she could stare daggers into his eyes. The sweat on her body was cooling fast, but she was angry enough to heat the whole building. "Did you follow me? Did you *break in*?"

"I heard you on the phone today, after you left the Chock'Lit Shoppe," he answered in a nervous undertone, glancing at the deadly gun barrel, "and I thought . . . I don't know, I thought you were in some kind of trouble. You said Dilton's death was your fault!"

"You let him *hear that*?" The woman gaped at Betty, her eyes wide. "What kind of amateur-hour nonsense—"

Betty sucked air in sharply through her nose. "You *eavesdropped* on my phone call, Archie? Really?"

"You were all upset! I just wanted to comfort you, and then—"

"That's it." The woman straightened back up again, aiming the gun at Archie's chest this time. "We're killing him."

"Stop that, nobody's killing anybody!" Betty fumed, shoving the woman's gun aside. "Look, I'm not any happier about this than you are, but we're here to *stop* the killing, remember?"

The woman still glared at Archie like she wanted to stomp him out with one of her heavy-duty boots, but she grudgingly holstered her weapon, and the boy breathed out a whimper of relief. "Betty, what's all this about? And who *is* this?"

Letting out a weary sigh, the blond girl said, "Archie, this is my aunt Elena Cooper. Aunt Elena, this is my neighbor Archie Andrews."

"This is your aunt?" Archie blinked.

At the exact same moment, Aunt Elena made a face. "This is the boy you said was cute?"

Suddenly, Betty's face alone was warm enough to heat the entire neighborhood, and she chose to ignore both questions. "This is a . . . it's kind of a private gym. My aunt owns it and runs it, and it's just for my family, so that we can train to fight—"

"Don't you dare finish that sentence, Betty Cooper," Aunt Elena snapped, holding up one long finger in warning. "I don't care how long you've known this kid, or how adorable you think his freckles are; your first duty is to this family, and you took an oath to protect our mission! What we do is classified."

"I took an oath to protect *innocent people*." Betty thrust a hand out at Archie, still huddled on the floor. "He already knows things he's not supposed to, and if I lie to him, how is he supposed to stay safe? Dilton was his friend, too, Aunt Elena, and the person behind this?" She bit her lip. "It's someone we both know. At this point, there's no good reason not to tell him the whole truth."

"Betty?" Archie stared up at her like he'd never seen her before. "What's going on? What do you mean, 'someone we both know'?"

"Archie." Betty took a breath and squared her shoulders. "This is going to be a lot for you to take in, so I need you to listen. The reason I'm here, the reason all of this is here, is because I'm training"—she hesitated, taking a deep breath—"to kill werewolves."

For a long moment, Archie didn't react at all. And then he scratched his head. "Werewolves."

"Yes." Betty shifted her weight awkwardly. She'd been expecting a somewhat more explosive response from him. "Werewolves. Like, from all the terrible movies? Only actually scary. What I'm saying is . . . they're real."

Archie's expression was still a total blank, and her frustration ratcheted up a notch.

"You do know what werewolves are, right? Humans shape-shifting under the full moon, growing lots of body hair, vulnerable to silver, all that stuff—"

"You think werewolves are real," Archie summarized carefully, his tone delicate and just vaguely condescending, as if he were speaking to someone in a straitjacket.

"I don't *think* they're real; I know they're real." Betty spoke through her teeth. "The Cooper family has hunted them for generations—it's what we do. It's been our mission since one of our ancestors encountered the first lycanthrope in these hills when he moved to the Riverdale area to work the lumber mills."

Archie scrunched up his brow. "Lichen throw-up?"

"*Lycanthrope*," Elena Cooper enunciated, rolling her eyes. "It's another word for werewolf, okay? Try to keep up."

In an undertone again, Archie asked, "Betty, is this some kind of cult? Do you . . . need help escaping?"

"You've got a lot of nerve, breaking in here and demanding answers that you refuse to believe." Elena thrust her chin at him. "This whole town would just be a forgotten tragedy in some local history book if it weren't for Elijah Cooper!"

Archie's brow scrunched a little more. "Uh . . . who?"

"My great-great-great-grandfather," Betty explained. "In the late nineteenth century, there were less than two thousand people living here, and a lot of them started dying in what looked like freak animal attacks. The whole town was in crisis, and the residents were talking about abandoning the area all together." With more than a trace of pride, she said, "Elijah was the one who finally managed to track the beast responsible—to learn what it really was—and he was the one who figured out how to kill it. Since then, the Cooper family has protected Riverdale from werewolves."

Archie looked from one of them to the other, and then he started to laugh. "Oh, I get it! You guys are mad because I snuck in, so now you're trying to prank me."

With an exasperated sigh, Betty set her jaw, coming to a decision. "Come on, Archie. There's something you need to see."

Grabbing him by the arm, she helped Archie to his feet and started walking him into the darkness beyond the obstacle course—toward another narrow hallway leading off from the makeshift gym. From behind them, Aunt Elena called out, her voice edged sharply with disapproval. "Elizabeth . . ."

"He can deny what he hears but not what he sees with his own two eyes," Betty called back over her shoulder—hoping it was true. Hoping she wasn't really making the huge mistake her aunt clearly believed she was.

The floodlights were so dazzling that leaving their reach was like venturing into deep space, the narrow hallway a black hole that closed around them with ominous totality. Betty knew the twists and turns of the corridor so well by now that she didn't even need to wait for her eyes to adjust, but she felt Archie's muscles tense up through the sleeve of his jacket. *Good.* At least he was taking this seriously.

The air at the head of the hallway smelled of dust, glue, and fresh paint; but the farther down it they walked, the thicker and muskier the odors became—rancid sweat, spoiling meat . . . and damp fur. There was a sound, too, a heavy, congested breathing that ruffled against the walls. When they were right up beside it, Betty finally stopped walking. "Okay, Archie. I'm going to turn on the light, and I need you to be ready, okay?"

He didn't say anything, so she flipped the switch, the sudden glare of overhead fluorescents making them both flinch. Before them stood a cage about the size of a stable, with thick metal bars that were bolted to the concrete floor, but what had Archie's undivided attention—his eyes huge—was the animal trapped inside. Massive and covered in patchy fur, with long limbs and paws the size of human hands, it was a wolf.

The beast snarled at the light, its narrowed eyes flashing a bright gold, its lips curled back to bare thick, monstrous teeth. Then, without warning, it lunged. One push from its muscular hindquarters launched it through the air, its massive body slamming against the bars right in front of Archie. The boy let out a strangled yelp of fright, jerking backward and stumbling into the wall behind him. But the bars held, the animal falling back, shaking itself off and growling deep in its throat.

"Bet-Betty," Archie gasped out, his face the color of oatmeal. "What . . . what the *hell*—"

"This is the real world, Archie." Betty spoke as calmly as she could while the beast paced inside its enclosure, showing off its dense muscle, its inhuman proportions. "*This* is what goes bump in the night. Werewolves are smart, deadly, and very, very real. A monster just like this one is what killed Dilton," she added darkly. "And it's still out there."

SEVEN

THERE WAS NO COUNTING THE number of students Geraldine Grundy had taught in the decades she'd worked at Riverdale High, and over the years, their names and faces had a habit of eroding from her memory. Some stood out, of course—for good reasons and for bad ones—but the pupils she would never, ever forget were those who had been lost too soon. That night, as she sat in her empty classroom, gazing out the broad windows at a lovely full moon, she knew Dilton Doiley would be forever etched into her memory.

Frankly, he was the kind of student she might have remembered anyway. His test scores had consistently been off the charts, his essays filled with information even she hadn't known, and he'd already taken enough college-level courses to skip his freshman year when he graduated. Maybe even to skip his sophomore year, as well. He had been a bright, perceptive boy with a promising future ahead of him, and it was everyone's loss that he would never fulfill his humbling potential. With his brain, who knew what discoveries he might have made?

Miss Grundy let out a heavy sigh and rubbed her eyes. It was honestly too sad to contemplate. Not that his intellect made his death more of a tragedy than if he'd been a *less* gifted student, like, say, Moose Mason, just for example. But the world always seemed to have plenty of boys like Moose to spare—those with more brawn than brains, preferring to solve their problems with childish violence rather than emotional maturity. It could have used another Dilton Doiley or two.

A cloud slid across the moon, its shadow slithering over the classroom floor, and for just a moment Miss Grundy sensed how alone she was at Riverdale High. When all the students left that morning, followed by the teachers and then the grief counselors, she alone had stayed behind. She'd said it was to catch up on grading papers—and she'd done a little of that, to be fair—but mostly it was because this classroom is where she felt closest to her students, and it seemed the best way to remember Dilton.

It was getting terribly late, though, and she was starting to nod off in her chair. It would be most embarrassing to get caught sleeping at her desk again, so Miss Grundy reluctantly pushed to her feet. She'd use the restroom one last time, collect her things, and head home. Dilton's memory would still be waiting here for her in the morning.

The cleaning staff was long gone, and the hallway was almost completely dark, shards of moonlight glancing in through high, narrow windows to create disorienting shapes on the opposite wall. Without people in it, Miss Grundy reflected, the school was tomb-like—hollow and foreboding, the shadows sinister in their stillness, the corridors ringing with a silence so thick it hurt the ears.

Unaccountably skittish, she used the facilities hastily, washed her hands, and started back up the twisting corridors to her classroom. When she got home, she'd find some mindless television show and probably fall asleep on the sofa with the cat curled up in her lap—the perfect end to a miserable day. She was already fantasizing about her thick slippers and flannel robe . . . when a faint sound brushed against her ear, and her footsteps faltered. Turning around, Miss Grundy peered into the darkness with a frown, more clouds disturbing the moon's faint, abstract illumination.

Just past the restroom, the hallway angled sharply to the left, concealing whatever lay beyond the bend. For a long moment, she stood rooted to the floor, listening. She was the only one left in the school . . . *wasn't she?* The sound, if she'd really heard anything at all, had been so indistinct she couldn't even describe it, and now that ringing silence was back in her ears again, her own breathing unnervingly loud. Miss Grundy licked her lips. "Hello?"

Her voice bounced down the darkened corridor and made the turn, fading into that eerie quiet, but the hair on the back of her neck rose anyway, her skin growing tight. Despite the silence, despite the vacant shadows and unsettling stillness, Geraldine Grundy suddenly knew beyond a shadow of a doubt that she was *not* alone—but someone wanted her to think she was. One more second passed as adrenaline prickled through her veins, and then she turned sharply on her heel and ran toward her classroom.

In her mind, she told herself that this was simple paranoia, a fearful hallucination brought on by a long, hard day of learning about the gruesome details of Dilton's death. But as she dashed up the corridor, her shoes slipping on the polished floor, she absolutely did not imagine the sound that came to life behind her. Feet pattered rhythmically, the click and skitter of nails against the tile amplified by metal lockers, the noise suggesting speed and weight.

Something was chasing her.

Fear sent another bolt of adrenaline screaming through her limbs, and Miss Grundy ran faster, too scared to look over her shoulder—even as she heard her pursuer skid around the bend in the corridor, even though she could already sense that the space between them was closing. Up ahead, the hallway made a sharp dogleg to the right, and her classroom was only another fifteen feet past the corner. If she could just make it inside, she could slam the door, lock it, and call the police. *She just had to make it.*

The noise behind her was getting louder, closer, feet slapping the ground with that terrifying *click-click, click-click*; it was an animal at full gallop, moving faster than Miss Grundy ever could—and just as she reached the dogleg in the hallway, she sensed the beast leaping into the air at her back.

Her heart in her throat, she ducked, gripping the brick wall and flinging herself around the corner a split second before the creature hurtled past her—close enough for the breeze to tickle her ear. There was a guttural yelp and a deafening crash of metal as the animal slammed full force into a row of lockers; but Miss Grundy was already racing for her open classroom, gasping for breath.

Heaving the door shut behind her, her chest on fire and her legs rubbery with fright, she just barely managed to twist the lock into place with quaking fingers before the beast caught up with her. It slammed into the frame from the other side with so much force the wood splintered, and Miss Grundy leaped back, a scream erupting from her throat. Two massive paws then appeared, pressed against the glass of the small window that looked out into the hallway . . . and then the creature's head rose into view.

Geraldine Grundy screamed again—and then a third time for good measure, tottering back, colliding with a student's chair and nearly losing her balance. The thing in the hall-way . . . it couldn't be real. It wasn't *possible*. Snarling and drooling on the other side of the glass was a wolf unlike any she'd ever seen before, standing at least six foot five on its hind legs, with fangs as long as fingers and impossibly glowing golden eyes. Its pink tongue slashed at the air, great globs of spittle raining down, and its throat worked as it produced a thick, rumbling growl. *"Grundyyyy . . ."*

She froze, the sound of her own name coming from the creature's jaws almost too shocking to process. A violent shudder raced along Miss Grundy's spine, and she gulped down a sob, telling herself all of this was a dream—it had to be. How could an animal like this exist, let alone find its way into the school? She'd fallen asleep at her desk again, and she would wake up, soon, any minute now. *Wake the hell up, Geraldine!* But as she watched, her eyes bulging with panic, the wolf threw its head back and howled.

High and hollow, the unearthly call filled the school's deserted hallways, echoing and building until it was as if a symphony of hellhounds were baying for her blood. Miss

Grundy backed farther away from the door, clapping her hands over her ears, tears streaming down her face.

But then a second howl rose to join the first, louder and clearer—because it was coming from the corner of the room at her back.

It was as she turned around, her joints stiff with fright, that Geraldine Grundy finally remembered something very important: Wolves hunt in packs. And she'd just let the one in the hallway drive her straight into a trap.

From behind her large wooden desk in the corner of the room, a second creature rose up from the floor, a wolf just as big as the one outside. Beneath its charcoal-and-silver pelt, thick muscle rippled across its massive shoulders, and with an effortless leap it sprang onto the desktop. It howled again, its cry echoed first by the wolf in the hallway and then at last by Miss Grundy's high-pitched, bloodcurdling wail of sheer terror.

And then the creature pounced.

EIGHT

THE CLOUDS HAD DISSIPATED, leaving a clear, dark sky, and Archie shivered all the way to his bones. The sight of a full moon had never been so disconcerting. His nostrils were still clogged with the putrid stench of werewolf breath, and he couldn't stop thinking about the way the creature in the cage had hurled itself against the bars, swiping at them with paws like dinner plates.

"Are you going to be okay to drive home?" Betty asked solicitously as she walked with him across the warehouse lot, Elena's music pumping again inside the building.

He decided to give her an honest answer. "I don't think I'm ever going to be okay again."

"It's overwhelming at first, I know." They stopped at the front gate, and she pulled out the key to the padlock, while Archie glanced across the street. He regretted parking in a shadow now. Before she undid the chain, Betty put a gentle hand on his arm. "You probably have a million questions."

He did, but only one came immediately to mind. "Werewolves are *real*?"

"Yup. Humans by day, monsters by the light of the full moon." Betty gave a shrug, as if it were all just that simple. "Some of them aren't even aware they're cursed—they just wake up the next morning thinking they had a bad dream and go on with their lives. The ones who know what they are, what they're doing . . . eventually, they can learn to control the shift."

That, at least, sounded hopeful. "So they can stay human?"

"So they can become wolves whenever they want to," Betty corrected grimly. "All lycanthropes change under the full moon, no matter what, because the nature of what they are is inescapable. But some of them enjoy it—they get off on the power and the viciousness." She glanced back at the warehouse, stark against the speckled night sky. "Shifting doesn't just affect them on a physical level. The more times they do it, the further they get from their humanity and the closer they come to the beast within. They stop caring about the carnage, and they don't want to feel guilty for it."

"Oh." Archie couldn't stop thinking about where his car was parked. It seemed a lot farther away than he remembered.

"So who was . . . who's that in your aunt's cage?"

Wrapping her arms around herself, Betty let out a troubled sigh. "My cousin Jacob. About five months ago, he got bitten while out on patrol, and now . . ." She gestures to the warehouse again. "Well, you saw him. He's his usual old self for all but three days a month, and then he turns into a nightmare that tries to eat people. His parents, my aunt and uncle, asked Elena to lock him up for safety, but . . . keeping werewolves in captivity isn't really a solution, either. They're incredibly strong, and they're as clever as they are deadly." Betty shook her head. "They also have unbelievable healing capabilities—some have been known to regenerate entire limbs. Put them in a cell and they'll slam themselves against the bars until either the metal gives or enough of their own bones shatter so they can squeeze through."

"But your cousin was—"

"The bars of that cage are coated with a paint containing silver dust, one of the werewolf's few fatal weaknesses; but tonight is the fourteenth time Jacob has shifted, and you saw how feral he's become. Sooner or later, his instincts will overtake him, and he'll do something drastic—like chewing off one of his own arms and using his blood to cover the paint."

At this, Archie made an expression of equal parts horror and disbelief, and Betty nodded.

"It's happened before. And that's the best-case scenario! The worst case is that he just stops coming, that he decides he doesn't want to be locked up on the full moon anymore, and his own family has to hunt him down."

Archie frowned. "Would you guys really do that?"

"We wouldn't have a choice," Betty answered promptly. "The only reason he's getting a shot at the cage in the first place is because his dad is in charge of our family's operations."

"But he's a normal guy, like, three-hundred-and-whatever days out of the year, though, right?" Archie protested. "Not to mention being, you know, *part* of the family operations."

He didn't mean it to come across in a scolding way, but Betty's face hardened just the same. "He's part of my family, yeah. But thirty-six days out of the year, he's the kind of guy who eats a campsite full of innocent college kids—or rips Dilton Doiley's head clean off his body. Look, Archie, the Coopers don't do this because it's *fun*; we do it because otherwise innocent people get slaughtered, or turned into monsters themselves! If a dog bites a child, it gets put down," she continued harshly. "It's an animal obeying its instincts, and if its instincts guide it to hurt people, then it's a danger to society. Period."

Archie shivered a little, discomfited by Betty's cold-blooded rhetoric. He understood what she was saying, and if he ever encountered a creature like the one he saw in Elena Cooper's cage, he knew he wouldn't be too particular about how it got stopped. But he couldn't help thinking about how, for three and a half weeks out of the month, that *thing* was the kind of guy who would volunteer to be caged so that he wouldn't hurt anyone. "But it's not like it's his fault this happened to him, right? I mean, obviously he doesn't want to be this way!"

"It's not about fault, or what anyone wants." Betty softened her tone. "*None* of us want this—but it's the way it is. Monsters come, and the Coopers stop them; because if we don't, there's no telling how many people could die. Whole towns could be destroyed. That's why we're out there, all over the country, continuing Elijah Cooper's mission—*because someone needs to fight back.*"

The picture she painted was alarming, and Archie squeezed his hands together, thinking again about Jacob Cooper's sharp teeth and massive claws—about the way the werewolf slammed himself against the cage over and over. Even the deadly paint on the bars hadn't so much as slowed him down in his urge to attack and kill.

"So how *do* you stop them?" Archie finally asked, his voice making an embarrassing squeak. "You said silver is one of their vulnerabilities . . . What are the others?"

"They don't have many," Betty answered darkly. "Aside

from silver, the only thing that seems to affect them is wolfsbane."

"Oh, of course, wolfsbane." Archie nodded thoughtfully. Then: "Uh . . . what's wolfsbane?"

"An extremely poisonous plant, lethal enough to kill a werewolf," she explained. "Historically, its toxin has been used for hunting and warfare purposes by different cultures, and we use it, too. It also acts as a natural repellent, in the same way that garlic is supposed to repel vampires—"

"Wait, *vampires* are real, too?"

"Archie! Focus!" Betty snapped her fingers a few times. "The *only* other vulnerability these creatures have is the complete destruction of their central nervous system, okay? Kill the brain, and the werewolf dies. Piano to the skull, bazooka to the face, cut their freaking heads off—whatever. It's primitive, but it works."

His stomach flopped over a few times. "H-have you done something like that before?"

Betty looked down at her feet for a moment before she answered. "I don't have any kills of my own, no. But the things I've seen while on patrol with my parents? I don't know if you're ready to hear about those."

Archie nodded distantly, and as he looked into her eyes, he realized that he didn't think he was ready for *any* of this. All this time, he'd been thinking of her as the girl he did puppet shows for from his bedroom window; meanwhile, she was training to fight monsters. "How do you do it, Betts? How do you face those things? And how do you learn to walk around and act like everything is normal when you know what's really out there?"

"Practice?" A tiny smile tugged at the corners of her mouth and then vanished when she saw he wasn't ready to joke yet. Cautiously she stated, "Werewolves aren't the only danger in the world, you know, Archie. I'm a girl—I spend every day assessing threats against my safety. At least these monsters are only a problem a few days a month."

He looked back to his car again, thinking of all the many nights he'd left the house without a second thought to go jogging, camping, hanging out with friends; all the times he'd gone for walks in the moonlight, thinking how peaceful and poetic it was. He had never once considered looking over his shoulder. For the first time, it really occurred to him that the women in his life were not quite as carefree as he was—that there were real dangers out there for them that he'd never have to worry about facing.

But now . . . knowing what he knew? He wanted a rear-view mirror installed on his forehead so he could never *stop* looking behind him. The night before, he'd taken the trash cans out to the curb for his dad, watching the fog move against the streetlights—while only a mile or so away, a man-wolf was getting ready to rip the entrails out of a budding valedictorian.

"Why here?" he asked next, unable to muster up much volume.

Betty cocked her head. "What do you mean?"

"You said your family's been doing this for generations, but . . . why Riverdale?" Archie elaborated, tossing his hands out to take in their surroundings. "I mean, it's not even that big of a town! How can there be enough werewolves around here to keep your family hunting them down for a hundred-and-whatever years?"

"I guess that's the other thing you really need to know," Betty acknowledged with a glum nod. "Lycanthropy . . . we call it a curse, but only because we don't really know a better way to describe it. All the old, familiar legends warn about the werewolf's bite—which is what turned my cousin Jacob—but the most common way for it to be transmitted is actually hereditarily."

"Hereditarily?" Archie wrinkled his brows.

"Through the blood. Through families." She turned her arm over, running a finger along the veins in her wrist. "It's a recessive gene, passed down from carriers to their children, and it asserts itself without any real predictability. It can happen to one sibling but not another; it can skip generations;

it can go dormant for hundreds of years, finally popping up out of nowhere in a family that didn't even know they bore the markers for it." Softly, sadly, she added, "No warning or anything. Just . . . one day you wake up and find out you're a monster."

"That's a really disturbing thought." Archie was chilled all the way to the bone. He tried to imagine what that would be like—to live a normal life until, overnight, you suddenly become a creature driven to commit the ghastly acts Betty was describing. It was petrifying, and he actually had no idea what he'd do if it happened to him. He didn't have an aunt with a free cage to spare. Would he want to live? *Would he want to die?*

"Don't worry," Betty said hastily, reading his mind. "Werewolf hunters keep meticulous records about this stuff, and I've looked up pretty much everyone in town. There's never been a known lycanthrope in either of your parents' family lines, at least as far back as I was able to trace them." It was exactly what he'd wanted to hear, and he sagged with unmitigated relief until she added, "But. The reason why werewolves are so prevalent in the region? Is because there are at least *four* established families here in Riverdale that we know carry the trait. And lycanthropy can be transmitted to humans even by the bite of a werewolf who's still in human form."

"Oh?" He *really* didn't like the sound of that.

"Wolves are pack animals, and they have a natural tendency to cluster geographically," Betty went on. "The good news—maybe the *only* good news—is that it's actually rare for the gene to assert itself, and even more rare for werewolves to deliberately make *new* werewolves just to have a pack. When they're in animal form, their instinct is to kill, not convert; and as humans . . . well, genetic lycanthropes tend to believe they're far superior to the ones who turn from a bite." She shrugged. "Basically, they're snobs. That's probably why, deep down, on a primitive level, families carrying the gene end up seeking one another out."

Goose bumps hardened the flesh on his shoulders as Archie remembered Betty's words from earlier in the night: *"It's someone we both know."* "Which families?"

"The Mantles, for one," Betty began, glancing around cautiously, as if they might be overheard in this desolate neighborhood on this lonely night.

"You mean it might be *Reggie*?" Archie sucked in a sharp breath, but then gave a slow nod. The more he thought about his chief rival at Riverdale High, the more reasonable the possibility sounded. "Actually, that makes a lot of sense. It would explain his attitude problem."

"Archie. Just because someone has an attitude—" Betty cut herself off, squeezing her eyes shut. "You know what?

Never mind. It might be him. It might also be one of the Blossoms."

Archie lifted his brows. "Cheryl and Jason Blossom also have this . . . lycra-thingy?"

"Lycanthropy. And I don't know for sure. All I can tell you is that their family carries the marker for it—Aunt Elena's records show a confirmed Blossom werewolf from sometime in the sixties." Betty crossed her arms over her chest. "But that means it could be anyone they're related to: parents, cousins, aunts, or uncles . . ."

"Yeah, but come on," Archie scoffed. "You *know* Cheryl. She's mean; she's athletic; she doesn't care about hurting people . . . You told me yourself she runs the cheerleading squad like a tyrant, right? If one of them is a werewolf, it's her."

"Maybe." Betty frowned, looking a little annoyed by his deductive process. "But if we're profiling people, then the one guy in Riverdale who really meets all the stereotypical werewolf criteria is Moose Mason—all quick-tempered, six foot infinity of him—and his family bears the curse as well."

"Really?" Archie's voice became embarrassingly thin. Moose was intimidating enough already, and a complete wrecking ball on the football field; imagining him with teeth and claws and an insatiable bloodlust was . . . not comforting.

"We can also add Bingo Wilkin to the list." Shifting uncomfortably, Betty wouldn't quite look Archie in the eye, and goose bumps spread clear to his elbows.

"Bingo? Jughead's *cousin* Bingo? Oh, man, that can't be . . ." Archie trailed off, hearing his own words, and his heart constricted. Licking his lips, he stammered, "W-why is Bingo on the list?"

Betty let out a terrible sigh, her shoulders drooping. "Because he has Jones blood in him. And the werewolf gene goes back centuries in Jughead's family."

"Wait—you don't . . . you can't . . ." Archie stepped back, letting out a bark of nervous laughter. "That's got to be some kind of a joke, right?"

"I really wish that it were." Her expression was grave, the corners of her mouth angled down.

"You can't possibly be suggesting that *Jughead freaking Jones* is—"

"I'm not suggesting anything," she stated flatly, but her tone was unconvincing. "I'm stating a fact, Archie. His family carries the gene. Aunt Elena has extensive records, and if you want, we can go right back inside and I can name every member of his family tree that's wolfed out and killed people at some point—"

"Stop, just stop it!" Archie put his hands up between them, taking a step back, his heart pounding. "I can't believe you. Jughead is our friend—*my best friend!*"

"And he might be innocent," Betty returned agreeably. "But, Archie . . . you need to be prepared for the possibility that he isn't."

"I'm not gonna listen to any more of this." Disgusted, Archie turned and yanked the chain free, shoving the gate open. "You've got your own cousin locked in a cage; you're talking about crushing people's skulls . . . I don't even know who you are!"

"You don't have to like it, but this is something you're just gonna have to deal with, Archie," she exclaimed in a fierce undertone, hurrying after him as he marched across the street. "Denial isn't going to protect you, and it isn't going to prevent more people from dying—trust me."

He ignored her, though, his ears burning with everything he wished he'd never heard, and just before they reached the driver's side of his car, Betty grabbed his elbow, stopping him in his tracks. "One of our friends might be the beast that killed Dilton, and I *will* stop them from hurting anyone else—no matter what it takes!"

👑👑👑

The sun was just coming up over the horizon, layering the sky in sherbet tones and splashing purple clouds with bright gold, when Jughead Jones opened his eyes. He was freezing cold, his head still heavy with sleep, and he was . . . naked? *Why was he naked?* For a groggy moment, he couldn't even figure out where he was. Rubbing his eyes, he sat up—and froze, his heart coming to a complete stop in his throat when he finally recognized his surroundings.

Headstones, blackened with age and studded with clumps of moss, poked out of the ground on either side of him; a marble angel knelt on a pedestal at his back, saying a silent prayer; and a gloomy mausoleum, its plinth reading JONES in block letters, stood directly before him. Bright yellow crime scene tape had been strung across the metal gate that guarded its doors, and Jughead gulped. He was in the *cemetery*; and was *this* exactly where Dilton had actually died? A wave of dizziness swept over him, the world pulsing with light, and he doubled over with his head between his knees.

His mind raced as he struggled to breathe, struggled to recall how he had possibly gotten here, but the last memory he could draw up was listening to music in Bingo's basement, laughing, surrounded by pizza boxes and soda bottles. Now he was in the graveyard—and he was *naked*. Was this a prank? Could his cousin have drugged him, taken his clothes, and dumped him at the foot of the family crypt as some kind of a joke?

"*Sheriff Keller was the first one on the scene when the grounds-keeper called the police.*" The memory of Veronica's words sent him scrambling to his feet, shivering all over with the cold. He had no idea what kind of hours the grounds-keeper kept, but there was no way he wanted to get caught stark naked in the middle of an actual crime scene, with grass and leaves stuck to his backside. He rubbed his eyes again, thinking—and that's when he finally noticed his hands.

They were filthy, with fresh dirt under his nails . . . but they were also covered in blood. His stomach rolled and heaved, and Jughead doubled over a second time, gagging up a thread of saliva that oozed into the grass. *This can't be happening.* His mouth had that same foul taste as the morning before, and he gasped for air, trying to fight the convulsions that tugged at his throat. Whatever was going on, he could figure it out later, but first he had to get home—before his mom came to wake him up for school and found him missing from his bed.

Ripping the liner out of a public trash can just next to the cemetery's side entrance, Jughead fashioned it into a make-shift smock, trying not to think about what had been inside of it before he'd emptied it onto the ground. He looked both ways before he sprinted up the road, his feet slapping the pavement, his garbage bag tunic fluttering in the morning breeze. No news crews, no dog walkers or early-morning joggers—the coast was clear. Even the streetlights were still on as he raced back home.

The metal brackets on the drainpipe cut his feet as he scaled the side of his house, clambering as quickly and quietly as possible onto the eaves near his bedroom window, and then tumbling inside. He was still shaking all over, his heart trying to punch its way through his rib cage, when he peeled off the liner and shoved it to the bottom of his wastebasket. He'd beaten his alarm by two minutes.

He was in the shower, desperately scrubbing dried blood from the creases in his palms, when the first uninvited memory came to him: Riverdale High, the hallways dark and empty; someone running, the air thickened by the smell of fear; a high-pitched scream mingling with the sound of . . . of—

"Forsythe?" His mom's voice, accompanied by a tentative knock at the door, broke through his train of thought. "Can I open the door?"

"I'm—I'm in the shower, Mom!" He tried to sound normal, but his voice was pitched an octave higher than it should be. "Can't it wait?"

There was a short pause, and then she spoke again. "It's important. There's been . . . Something's happened."

"Okay, okay," he replied hastily, scrubbing up one last

time before shutting off the water. The blood was still there, still clinging to the tiny grooves over his knuckles, the razor-thin lines that made hatch marks in the webbing of his thumbs. Grabbing a thick terry-cloth robe off a hook on the wall, Jughead shrugged into it before he opened the door, burying his hands in the deep pockets. "What's going on?"

He was so preoccupied with his own problems that it took him a moment to realize how pale his mother was, her skin almost waxy under the light from the hall as she said, "School's been canceled again today, honey."

She was staring at him as if trying to memorize all the lines on his face, like maybe she'd never see him again, and he froze under the scrutiny.

Dumbly, he managed, "It has?"

"I was going to let you sleep, but then I heard the water running, and—" Her words choked off abruptly, and she swallowed, shaking her head. "I just didn't want you to find out from the news."

"Why not?" he demanded.

His mind was still racing, casting out feelers in all directions, trying to fill the void that stretched between Bingo's basement and the family crypt, trying to make sense of yet another horrible dream. He'd woken up naked in a graveyard, covered in blood, and now class was canceled

for the second day in a row? It couldn't be a coincidence—
and yet it *had* to be a coincidence. *Please, please let it be a coincidence.*

"It's a day off, right?" In the pockets of his robe, his bloodied hands throbbed with guilt. "Who cares how I find out
about it?"

"It's because of the reason," Mrs. Jones answered with a
tremulous sigh, and the hollow, worried look in her eyes hit
him like the front end of a truck. "I don't know how to tell
you this, Forsythe . . . but one of your teachers was killed
last night. And it happened on school property, so the building is a crime scene."

The ground dropped away from beneath him. *Dark, empty
hallways; someone running; the air thickened by the smell of fear.* His
voice squeaking, Jughead asked, "Wh-who was it?"

"Miss Grundy." His mom rubbed her mouth and swiped
a tear from the corner of her eye. "I'm so sorry, honey.
They're saying . . . apparently it was another animal
attack, like what happened to your friend Dilton. They
don't know how wild animals could have gotten into the
school, but—"

"*Into* the school?" Jughead repeated in a daze, his hands
tingling now in the pockets of his robe. *Howling.* A high-
pitched scream mingled with the sound of *howling.*

A sob burst from his mother, tears rolling down her

cheeks, and she pressed her hands together. "They're saying . . . they're saying she was *eaten*."

The room flickered, his stomach inverted, and Jughead barely made it to the sink in time to hurl chunks of half-digested meat into the drain.

NINE

NOTHING MADE ARCHIE FEEL more invincible than a fit of righteous anger, but when he woke up the next morning to the news of another gruesome attack by the Riverdale Ripper, he felt nothing but overwhelming guilt. *Miss Grundy was dead.*

The shock of it was like falling through ice—a sudden, cold bath that snapped him out of his sense of moral superiority. Betty had been putting herself through the paces in her aunt's obstacle course, getting both mentally and physically ready to face down a monster, and Archie had been thinking up creatively mean-spirited things to say about her disloyalty. One after another, he'd devised brilliant, if tardy, comebacks to her suggestion that *Jughead Jones* might be responsible for what happened to Dilton.

Meanwhile, a killer—most likely someone they knew—had been ripping Miss Grundy apart.

The reports of what had happened at Riverdale High the night before were vague, but in a way, what they didn't say was worse than what they did. Archie's imagination worked overtime, remembering all the horrible things Reggie had described at the Chock'Lit Shoppe the previous afternoon, but now picturing them being done to his teacher. The truth was that Archie had gotten on Miss Grundy's bad side a lot more than he'd ever been on her good side—usually for not paying attention in class, or forgetting to do his homework. But all the times that he'd cursed her name under his breath after getting a bad grade on a test weren't what came back to him as he tried to make sense of the morning's headlines.

He remembered that she had a cat—a rescue—that she'd once had to treat for ear mites. He remembered her laughing about the singles' cruise she once went on for her birthday and how it turned out that the only thing she didn't like about the trip was having to share the boat with other people. Most of all, he remembered that she would wistfully call Riverdale High her "home away from home." He'd thought it was sad, at the time, all these lonely-sounding things; but looking back, he realized how genuinely happy she'd seemed while talking about them. She wasn't just some robot that turned on when the first bell rang—she was a person with a life and interests of her own. And now she was dead.

After a long run failed to clear either his mind or his conscience, Archie swallowed his pride and made a call. Betty picked up on the second ring, but he didn't wait for her to say hello before launching into what was on his mind. "Listen, I'm sorry about the things I said last night. You were right—"

"Forget it." Her tone was firm but understanding. "It's pretty awful stuff to know about, and you're not the only one who's freaked out over what it all means, you know?"

"It's just going to keep happening, isn't it?"

"Until someone stops the beast. Well, until *I* stop it," Betty said. "Aunt Elena has her hands full with my cousin— his parents are on the other side of the country, and *my* parents are mostly retired from the game at this point." She let out a heavy sigh. "Did you hear that school is canceled indefinitely?"

Archie nodded before he realized that she couldn't see him over the phone. "On TV they said the crime scene was so bad that it could take days for the police to process it."

Betty made some noises with her mouth. Then: "Reggie is having a party tonight."

"What?" Archie stared at the phone. *This* was news. "He's . . . *what*?"

"According to the text blast he sent out it's 'in honor of Dilton and Miss Grundy,'" Betty reported, apparently reading out loud from the message. "But really it's a 'spring break in September' party. Since we 'might have a whole week off, now. On account of all the carnage and stuff.'"

Archie's nose wrinkled back until it practically touched his forehead. "Two people just died! What's wrong with him?" Then: "And did he seriously not invite me?"

"He's Reggie," she answered with a verbal shrug. "Anyway, I don't know if you have plans tonight, but it'll be down by the river—near the Wesley Road bridge—and it starts at ten."

He waited for her to say she was making some kind of a tasteless joke, and when she didn't, he demanded, "You're not serious, right?"

"Archie. This is the third night of the full moon, and a whole bunch of our friends are going off into the woods to make noise and be irresponsible." Her words were crisp, edged in impatience. "It's exactly the same recipe that led to those campers being slaughtered last month, and I'm not going to let that happen again. If Reggie's having a party, I'm going to be there. I have to—it's my job."

"Oh." He stopped, silent for a moment. "I . . . hadn't thought of it that way."

"I get it if you want to stay home," she said next, her tone softening. "This isn't your responsibility, and things could get . . . hairy. Literally. But I'll never forgive myself if I *don't* go and something happens to anyone else we care about."

Archie was unsettled for the rest of their conversation, unable to say he'd go and unable to say he wouldn't. The whole idea of partying right now grossed him out, but Betty was right: Everyone who attended could be in danger. And it's not like he could just come right out and *warn* them. They would laugh him out of town if he tried to tell people that there was a *werewolf* on the loose. What really bothered him is that he shouldn't have to warn anybody about anything; people were getting killed! Whether it was a supernatural monster, some feral animal, or just a run-of-the-mill, ax-wielding drifter—who still wanted to go hang out in the woods?

The people going to this party probably thought safety in numbers would protect them. The authorities were still being cagey about what exactly had gone down with Miss Grundy, but everyone knew she had been alone when she was killed—just like Dilton was. Besides, Reggie had thrown tons of parties by the Wesley Road bridge, where the river bent and a vast expanse of flat rocks backed up to the tree line, and nothing bad had ever happened. A bunch of campers dying in the no-man's-land between Riverdale and Midville probably wasn't on anybody's radar.

More and more, it was starting to look like Betty Cooper might be their only hope.

ᘓᗯᘓ

For a while after she finished talking to Archie, Betty lay on her back in bed, staring at the ceiling. Dark clouds pressed in on her thoughts, and she did her best to push them back, but it was something of a losing fight.

Battling werewolves was a duty she'd spent her whole life preparing for, from reading the lore and studying combat techniques, to field training with her family. She was thirteen the first time she'd been handed a gun loaded with live ammunition—bullets she'd cast herself with molten silver—and told she'd be participating in a real-life hunt. There'd been a possible sighting in the woods outside a town in her parents' sector, and the Coopers needed to check it out.

It had been a false alarm in the end, but the entire experience had been a rush—terrifying and exhilarating all at once. She knew then that she wanted to be ready, to be worthy of this calling, so that one day when the time came, she could lead a mission of her own.

Their family tree had grown considerably since Elijah Cooper's day, with branches now spreading throughout the country, and everywhere there were Coopers to be found there were hunters. Each unit tried to ensure that there was at least one member actively tracking and confronting the lycanthrope menace, with territories carefully staked out. Riverdale, being the starting place and unofficial head-quarters of the operation, had benefited over the years from having multiple full-time hunters in play at any given time.

Or, at least, that used to be the case. But over the years, Betty's mother's eyesight had gotten to the point where she was no longer a reliable shot, and a back injury her father suffered the previous year had made it necessary for him to step down. With Polly away at school, Betty still inexperienced, and no other Coopers close enough to take on the work, Elena and Jacob had added managing the Riverdale territory to their responsibilities in Greendale and Midville. Things had been working out just fine . . . until now.

The bite that took Jacob out of commission had also resulted in a full-moon babysitting job for Elena, which meant that almost the entire region was going virtually unprotected. For months, Betty had been worried about a werewolf attack, and when those campers had been killed, she knew—she *knew*—it was her worst fears come true. And still she'd rebelled against everything her instincts and her common sense were telling her, because deep down she was scared that she wasn't ready to face the monsters alone.

Betty was still scared. And maybe she *wasn't* ready. But she had to step up to the plate, because, ready or not, there was no one else. This was her mission—the first mission where she'd be the one calling all the shots—and now was her chance to prove that she could be worthy of the Cooper name and everything it stood for. No matter what, she had to come through, and she had to stop the beast that was stalking Riverdale. Even if it meant hunting one of her friends. Even if it meant killing one of them.

Betty closed her eyes and pushed as hard as she could against those dark clouds. She had a party to get ready for.

♛♛♛

It was after nine when his cell vibrated with an incoming call from Jughead, and Archie momentarily froze. They'd texted a couple of times throughout the day, but he still couldn't quite get over what Betty had said the night before, about the werewolf gene passing down through the Jones family line. It was ridiculous; Jughead was the gentlest guy in Riverdale, and anybody who knew him could attest to it. The guy captured bugs and set them free outside so he wouldn't have to squash them, for Pete's sake! And yet Archie's mouth was dry when he finally answered the phone.

"Hey, man, what's up?"

"Hey." There was a pause on the other end of the line, Jughead breathing awkwardly into the speaker. "Um . . . did you hear that Reggie's throwing some kind of party tonight?"

"Yeah, I heard." Archie sighed, rubbing his face. "It's disrespectful as hell, if you ask me."

At the exact same moment, Jughead asked, "Any chance you could drive me there?"

"What?" For the second time that day, Archie was sure he was hearing things. "You seriously want to go? Don't you think the whole idea is kinda messed up?"

Silently, he promised himself that Jug wasn't asking because he was a secret werewolf and needed a ride to the all-you-can-eat Riverdale High buffet; surely, he had some other reason. "Reggie's parties always suck anyway."

"I mean, you're not wrong, it's just . . ." Jughead trailed off for a moment. "I heard a bunch of kids from Midville are supposed to be there, and I've been trying to reach my cousin Bingo all day. There's something really important I need to talk to him about."

"You want to go to Reggie's dirtbag party because your cousin isn't answering his texts." Archie wasn't trying to sound insulting, but his tone had a sharper edge than he intended.

"It's really important," Jughead repeated, and then silence filled the line.

It was a moment before Archie could figure out how to respond.

"Do you honestly think it's a good idea?" Archie was nervous and practically pleading with his best friend to change his mind, to avoid everyone and stay out of trouble until the full moon was past. There were a lot of things he could say here, but many more that he couldn't. What if—*what if*—Jughead really was the beast that Betty was after? Archie hated even thinking that way, but he wanted his best friend as far from any danger as possible . . . no matter which side of the danger he was on. "People are dying out there, Jug! Maybe we should both just stay home tonight."

Jughead let out a heavy sigh. "Forget it. I'll take my bike—"

"Don't do that; that's dumb. This thing is all the way on the other side of town!" Archie gritted his teeth, trying to bite back the words that were about to come out of his mouth. "I can drive."

It was everything he didn't want to do, but if Jug was going anyway, Archie couldn't let him go alone. He could watch the guy, make sure nothing happened—clear his name and narrow Betty's list of targets. Mostly he just couldn't imagine sitting at home like a coward, keeping himself safe while everyone else was out in the woods, their lives in danger from something he knew about and they didn't. Anyway, it was already after dark, and the full moon was out; if Jughead was a werewolf, wouldn't he have already transformed by now?

His parents would surely have refused to let him leave the house, so Archie waited until they went to bed and then snuck out behind their backs, guilt rattling around in the pit of his stomach. With the exception of lying about unfinished homework, dishonest acts always gave him indigestion, because he couldn't shake the certainty that he was going to get caught. This anxiety plagued him all the way to the Joneses' house, where his best friend barely even acknowledged his moral anguish. Jughead was unnaturally quiet when he got in the car—shrugging off conversation attempts, or mumbling one-word answers until there was nothing left to say—and they made the trip to Reggie's party in near total silence.

Lights flashed through the trees, music thumping in the air from portable speakers, as they parked just off Wesley Road. Technically a county highway, it cut through the woods and crossed the river via a classic covered bridge, ultimately leading to Midville. Reggie Mantle wasn't the first person to throw a party on the flats along the embankment here—but if Betty was right, he might be the last.

They had just reached the clearing at the water's edge, the noise getting louder and more distinct, a throng of shadows taking on shape and recognizable features, when someone shouted, "ARCHIE ANDREWS!"

A petite blonde barreled through the crowd, shoving people out of the way and leaping through the air to land in Archie's arms, liquid sloshing out of a red plastic cup in her hand. She yelped, hiccupped, and then giggled loudly in his ear. "You came!"

"Betty?" Archie eased her to the ground, holding her out at arm's length, staring. "Are you . . . have you been *drinking*?"

"What, this?" She indicated her cup with exaggerated offense, making a face and blowing air through her lips. "This is a *libation*, Archie, it's very different. It's more suspisticat—sophomistic—susurra—"

"Sophisticated?"

"*That's* it! That's the one." Betty touched her nose with a coy wink.

Archie was still staring at her, his disappointment warring with his disbelief, when Jughead interrupted them. "I'm gonna find my cousin."

"Jug, wait—" But before Archie could disentangle himself from Betty, his best friend had already vanished into the crowd. It looked like half their school had turned out, and the riverside was clogged with bodies. Letting out a frustrated grunt, Archie exclaimed, "Are you kidding me, Betts? You're actually . . . *partying*? What if, what if . . ."

Only he couldn't finish the question, because even with the blasting music, even with the buzzing din of conversation, there was no way to say the word *werewolf* without the risk of being overheard.

Swatting his chest with a loose, rubbery hand, Betty stated, "You need to go get a libation and *relax*, Archie. We only get one spin on the big blue marble, so you might as well have fun!"

"I cannot believe you—" he started to say, but before he could finish, she had already shoved him aside, charging at a new group of people emerging from the trees.

"RONNIE!" Betty shrieked excitedly, tackling Veronica Lodge and nearly bringing them both to the ground.

Shaking his head in disgust, Archie spun around, stomping deeper into the mob. If Betty couldn't be counted on, then it was more important than ever that he keep an eye on Jug . . . only the guy was nowhere to be seen. There were people all over the place, pushing in from every side, and despite the full moon and the intermittent camera flashes that pulsed regularly up and down the flats, he couldn't see his best friend anywhere.

Anxiety brushed its fingers over Archie's skin as he turned in circles, looking for Jughead's distinctive hat—wondering what he actually thought he was going to do to keep people safe if the worst really happened. No matter what kind of mental state she was in right now, Betty had trained for this; he'd watched her do acrobatics and take impossible shots, hitting a bull's-eye without even aiming. Meanwhile, he'd barely been able to climb over a fence without breaking his ankle, and he'd gotten his butt soundly handed to him by Elena Cooper because he didn't know the first thing about actual combat.

The truth was, Archie realized, his shoulders sinking in dismay, that if a werewolf attacked Reggie's party? He would be nothing but a liability. One more body to be reported on the news; his parents left to grieve and wonder where they'd gone wrong, why they hadn't paid more attention the night he snuck out to make a bad decision for good reasons.

Archie stood in place for nearly a minute longer, coming to a decision, then he turned back around again. He was useless here and should never have come to begin with. Marching through the trees, he got into his car and cranked the engine, pulling a U-turn and heading for town. Jughead and Betty were on their own; there was something he needed to do.

♛♛♛

Someone had brought a grill, and the smell of meat roasting over hot coals drifted in the chilly air. Jughead's stomach clamped down, his gorge rising, and he swallowed compulsively against the roiling queasiness. He should never have come here. Ever since he'd vomited into the bathroom sink that morning, eating had proven an impossible chore, and more of his terrible dream from the previous night had surfaced. Moonlight on metal lockers, blood and twitching limbs, Miss Grundy's scream rising to a hideous harmony with that unearthly *howling*.

It couldn't be real—there was no *way* it could be real—but Bingo had been dodging his calls and texts all day, and the situation was driving him out of his mind. Jughead needed to know how he'd ended up in the cemetery, naked and covered in blood, haunted by detailed visions of yet another death. There *had* to be an explanation, and his cousin was the only person who might be able to give it to him.

Closer to the water, the crowd got more boisterous. Guys in varsity jackets were "jokingly" threatening to throw a weedy-looking underclassman into the river, and Jughead steered the other direction. He studied faces on the periphery of the gathering—some strange and some familiar, but none of them Bingo—and then slipped into the trees. Some intuition he couldn't name was pulling at him, an invisible thread guiding him away from the noise and toward a quieter stretch of the embankment. He itched beneath his skin, his legs jumpy, and he briefly fantasized about running all the way home just to satisfy them.

When he emerged from the woods again, farther down the river, he nearly stumbled right over a couple sitting on a wide, flat rock that formed a shelf above the water. They were kissing—aggressively—their faces grinding together with a wet, smacking noise, and Jughead reflexively apologized for intruding before either of the pair was even aware of his presence. "Whoops! Sorry, I didn't mean to—*Bingo?*"

The boy on the rock broke the kiss and looked up with a lazy smile, not seeming at all surprised by Jughead's sudden arrival. "Hey, cousin. I was wondering when you'd get here."

"I, uh . . . I was looking for you, but I don't want to interrupt, or whatever," he stammered, still feeling awkward. And then Bingo shifted, moonlight falling on the girl beside him, and Jughead started when he recognized Ethel Muggs.

"Hey, Juggie." She gave him a shy smile, her lips swollen and pink, a dreamy, contented look smeared all over her face. "It's nice to see you."

"Yeah, sure, um . . . you too." Jughead adjusted his hat, trying to figure out where to put his eyes. For a while there, he'd been pretty sure Ethel was into *him*, and although the feelings hadn't been mutual, the circumstances here still felt really strange. "How long have you two . . . known each other?"

"We met a couple months ago, but we didn't really *know* each other until tonight," Bingo said, smoothing out the collar of the girl's jacket. "Right, Ethel?"

She giggled, giving him back a besotted look. "I really like his band."

"Why were you looking for me?" Bingo asked next, his eyes still on Ethel, and it took Jughead a moment to realize who the guy was speaking to.

Clearing his throat, he mumbled, "It's . . . kind of, um, personal?"

Bingo glanced up again, his expression unreadable, but after a moment he said, "Hey, Ethel, you don't mind giving me and Jughead a little privacy, do you?"

"No, of course not." The girl got up, brushing off the seat of her pants, running her fingers through her hair to smooth out the fresh tangles. "I'll go see if I can find Midge and the others."

"Thanks, babe, you're the best," he called after her as she headed into the trees. "I'll call you!"

Ethel giggled again, tossing a little wave back over her

shoulder, and then she was gone. Bingo slapped his hand down on the rock beside him, right where the girl had been sitting a moment ago. "Take a load off, cousin, tell me what's on your mind."

He'd been looking for Bingo, of course, but now that they were alone together, the questions didn't want to come out of Jughead's mouth. He sat down obediently, his hands clutched in sweaty fists, and took a steadying breath before blurting, "What happened last night?"

"You came over. You don't remember?" Bingo's question was almost too casual.

"Of course I remember, but I don't . . ." Only, how could he possibly finish that statement? Maybe he *was* losing his mind. If he told Bingo that he'd blacked out and woken up naked and bloody in a graveyard, maybe he'd end up in an institution somewhere. "Just answer me, okay? What did we do when I came over?"

"Well, let's see." Bingo gazed up at the moon, showing bright and full through a thin lace of clouds. "We ordered pizza, watched a movie, you listened to my band's new song— you said it was really great, by the way, and that we totally deserve a recording contract. I want to make sure you remember that part."

"Yeah, okay, and then what?" Jughead rotated his hand impatiently.

"Then you were hungry again, and we decided to go out to eat." The moonlight threw deep shadows across Bingo's hooded eyes as he turned to face his cousin. "So we changed and came back to Riverdale."

This was the part he still couldn't remember, no matter how hard he tried, and Jughead squirmed in nervous antici-pation. The itch beneath his skin was getting worse. "Where did we go? What did . . . what did we eat?"

"We went to your school," Bingo answered serenely, his eyes still engulfed by shadow, "and we ate your teacher."

A breeze gusted along the river, carrying a swell of voices from Reggie's party, and Jughead gripped the edge of the rock to keep from toppling into the river. "Th-that's not funny, man. What the hell is wrong with you? Don't say stuff like that!"

"I think the question you really want to ask me is what the hell is wrong with *you*." A corner of Bingo's mouth ticked up in a smirk, more clouds flitting across the moon. "After all, you were the one who knew how to get into the building after hours, because of some unsecured hatch on the roof," he continued, "and you were the one who chased good old Miss Grundy right into the trap we set."

Jughead lurched to his feet, his heart racing so fast his lips tingled. "I don't know what you're talking about, but . . . but you need help, Bingo. This is . . . this is—"

"This is who you are, *cousin*." Bingo cut him off, on his own feet in the time it took Jughead to blink, a strange light gleaming in his shadowed eyes. "Last night we hunted down your teacher; the night before that, it was your buddy Dilton in the cemetery; and last month, we had a bona fide smorgasbord in the woods, thanks to those campers." His smirk pulled into a grin, his sharp teeth suddenly on display. "That was the best meal I've had in a long time—and you didn't exactly complain, either."

"*Stop*. You can't . . . this isn't . . ." Jughead's stomach revolted again, bile crawling up the back of his throat, and he couldn't finish. The dreams he'd been having—the blood, the screams, the people running for their lives; the way he'd woken up those mornings with a full stomach and grimy teeth, unfamiliar dirt trapped under his fingernails—they were all forming a picture that he didn't want to see. It was horrifying and unthinkable, something that couldn't possibly be true . . . and yet it *felt* true.

That was the worst part of all. It was as if Bingo had reached right into the darkest, most disturbing part of his mind and ripped his fears clean out like a still-beating heart so he could play with them. How could he possibly describe Jughead's dream about chasing Miss Grundy so accurately? Or even know about the one with Dilton in the cemetery? Bingo's explanation landed like a gut punch, and everything seemed to spin around them.

"We're werewolves, Jughead," Bingo went on, saying the word as easily as he might have said *bookworms* or *Scorpios*, gripping his cousin by the lapels of his jacket. "Thanks to the full moon and the blood of the Jones family, we are something far better than a bunch of pitiful, sad-sack humans. It usually kicks in after puberty, and I've been waiting a full year for you to come into your gifts."

"There's something wrong with you." Jughead could hardly breathe. "If this is some kind of sick, twisted joke—"

"You know how I knew you'd show up here tonight?" Bingo's voice was smooth as cream. "Because the full moon is up, and your instincts kicked in, telling you to seek out the rest of your pack."

"I came here because I woke up naked in a graveyard this morning, and the only guy who knows what happened to me last night was leaving all my texts on read!" Jughead struggled to break the iron grip his cousin had on his jacket. "But obviously your brain is broken, because people I know have *died* and you're joking about . . . about—"

"I get it, buddy. You don't remember anything yet. I freaked out, too, when I first started to change, and for months my brain blocked out everything that happened on the full moon." He brought his face closer, that light in his eyes burning brighter. "But you feel it, right? The way your skin doesn't fit right tonight? The way you're hungry for something but all this junk food just makes you want to hurl?" Bingo pressed his lips right up against Jughead's ear, murmuring, "It'll come back to you soon, cousin, I promise. And just wait till you remember how good it felt when you tore Dilton Doiley's throat out with your teeth."

Emitting a strangled shout, Jughead swung his fist at Bingo's face; but the boy danced back out of reach on nimble feet, laughing with delight as the punch missed his jaw by inches. Jughead was just taking a step forward, confused rage building in his chest, when a figure burst suddenly out of the trees. Leaping at Bingo, the blond girl wrapped her arms and legs around him from behind, shrieking wildly.

"BINGO WILKIN!"

Without missing a beat, Jughead's cousin did a graceful spin, while Betty Cooper hooted and giggled, something splashing around in her red plastic cup. When they stopped, she slid to the ground again, her steps unsteady and her face flushed. Reaching up, she ruffled Bingo's hair, and the boy grinned down at her.

"Well, hey there, BC."

"It's my favorite musician!" Betty warbled happily, her drink spilling as she swept her arms out. "Look, Juggie, it's my favorite musician!"

"I see him," Jughead snapped, breathing hard. He wanted Betty to go away so he could shake some answers out of his cousin, but all his words were knotted up in his throat.

"I like it when a pretty girl calls me her favorite." Bingo took Betty's hand and guided her in a neat little pirouette, the moonlight making her hair shine.

"And this girl likes it when she gets a compliment from Wingo Bilkin." Making a face, Betty tried again. "Binko Wigpin. Wiggo Pigpen."

She dissolved into paroxysms of laughter, and Bingo deftly slipped the plastic cup out of her hands, dumping the rest of its contents onto the rocks at their feet.

"Hey!" Betty yelped, watching the remains of her drink vanish. "Awww."

"Sorry, Betty, but you'll thank me in the morning," Bingo said, tugging gently on her ponytail. "I think you've probably had enough of whatever was in there already."

"It was a *libation*." She winked at him conspiratorially, and then patted his face.

"So it was." With another deft move, he reached into Betty's pocket and slipped out her car keys, tossing them at his cousin without warning. Jughead swiped them out of the air single-handed, scowling furiously, while Bingo said, "Cuz, I believe the lovely Miss Cooper could use a driver to see her home safely."

"But the party's not over yet!" Betty protested with a pouting frown, twisting a ring around her middle finger.

"But your favorite musician's about to leave, so it won't be fun for much longer anyway," Bingo returned smartly.

Jughead was rooted to the ground as his cousin headed for the trees, calling back in a playful voice, "You look a little pale tonight, Jughead. Maybe you and Betty should stop for a bite on the way home."

And then he was gone, leaving Jughead all alone with Betty beneath the full moon—and the faintest beginnings of a hungry growl building in his stomach.

TEN

THE MUSIC SHE'D PICKED tonight was bass-heavy, the beat relentless, thudding like an external heartbeat as she stretched her limbs. The obstacle course had been rearranged from the night before, with new targets and a few extra challenges thrown in for good measure—because despite the late hour, Elena Cooper was antsy, and she needed to blow off steam. Jacob had shown up ten minutes past sundown, sullen and drunk, and she could practically smell the beast fighting to surface inside him as she'd taken him to his cell.

He wouldn't return at the next full moon; she already knew it. She could see the conflict in his eyes—the shame over what he'd become warring with his fear over what would surely happen if he made the wrong move while under her watch—and before long, he'd be making plans to run. Which meant she would have to go after him. Taking a swig from her water bottle, Elena started the timer and launched into the course.

She was halfway through—a dozen targets down—and not even out of breath yet, when she heard it: an insistent pounding, so loud it broke through both the pulsing music and the thick membrane of her concentration. For a moment, Elena thought it was Jacob, having finally lost his last bit of self-control, trying to break out of his cage. But then she oriented herself in the center of the obstacle course and realized the sound was coming from the front door.

Two heartbeats passed as she stood there, thinking. Aside from Jacob, the only people with any business walking onto the warehouse lot—who even knew this place was here—already had keys to that door. Whoever her uninvited guest was, they had circumvented a padlocked gate, and they hadn't called ahead to say they were coming.

Swiftly, Elena Cooper cast aside her harmless paint pistols and reached for her real sidearm—the Smith & Wesson Model 500, loaded with custom silver bullets, that was never more than a few paces away from her at all times. It was a bear of a gun, capable of stopping anything up to and including a werewolf with a single shot, and not for the inexperienced or faint of heart. The first time she'd fired it, the recoil had nearly dislocated her shoulder.

Leaving the music on, Elena crept almost silently through the shadows to the front entrance, the pounding getting louder. A computer screen beside the door showed the view of a night-vision surveillance camera mounted outside, and Elena's eyebrows hitched upward when she took in the identity of her mysterious visitor. Tossing open the locks, she greeted him with the barrel of her weapon, glaring down the length of her nose. "Hate to break it to you, but your girlfriend's not here tonight, Coppertop."

"I know," Archie Andrews said, his face cast half in shadow by the light of the full moon. To his credit, he barely flinched at the sight of her gun. (This time.) "I came to see you."

"Oh?" She arched a brow, taking in his hunched shoulders and nervous body language, lowering her weapon. He wasn't a threat. "Well, I guess I'm flattered, but you're not exactly my type."

"Not because of—" The boy caught himself when he seemed to realize she was joking. Setting his jaw, he grunted, "I want you to teach me. About werewolves. I want . . . I want to be able to do what Betty does."

Both of Elena's eyebrows went up this time. "She's been training most of her life to do this stuff—it doesn't just happen overnight. And anyway, have you really thought this through, kid? We don't fight werewolves for the laughs, you know. We do it because they kill people if we don't. Sometimes they kill *us*."

"Two people I know are dead already," Archie replied, his tone grave and considered, "and the monster that did it is still out there. What if the next victim is someone I can't bear to lose? What if . . . what if it's Betty, because she's the only one who knows how to face these things?" Squaring his shoulders, he lifted his chin, meeting her eyes. "I want to help."

Elena grinned, running a hand through her dark hair— deliberately pulling it out of her face so he could see the three jagged lines of scar tissue that cut across her cheek. It was a souvenir she would always have from her first kill. She'd let the beast get too close and learned an agonizing lesson. "You make a persuasive case, Archie Andrews. Come on in."

♛♛♛

The drive home from Reggie's party seemed to take twice as long as it should have, the car filled with uncomfortable silence, and Betty spent most of the ride staring out the window at the bright eye of the moon. Just as he had been the previous morning at the Chock'Lit Shoppe, Jughead was distracted and fretful, his knuckles white around the steering wheel. She wanted to ask what was on his mind, but she was afraid to hear what his answer might be.

The only reason she went to the party in the first place was to hunt for a killer, to protect her friends, and now she felt like she was failing in her mission. All she'd managed to do was confuse herself and risk compromising the very objectivity that she'd preached to Archie about the night before. She had always taken pride in her ability to think of werewolves as monsters, first and foremost; but how could she now, when all the suspects were her friends?

Reggie Mantle was undeniably an ass—but he'd completely surprised Betty with his behavior that night.

When one of her favorite songs had started playing on the speakers by the water's edge, Betty had whooped with glee, charging for the makeshift dance floor. Eyes closed and drink aloft, she'd twirled and swayed to the music, letting it wash over her, losing herself in the melody. And then she felt someone's hands touching her waist, and when she opened her eyes, she found some creep from Midville—a guy she'd never even met before—trying to grind up against her. Grossed out, she shoved him away . . . which made him mad.

Before the moment boiled over, however, Reggie had intervened. Red with rage, he'd gotten right in the face of the Midville kid, shouting at him for trying to take advantage of a girl who'd been drinking, and then he threw *the creep* and *his friends* out of the party.

When he was sure they were really leaving, he turned, looping his arm around Betty's shoulders and giving her a side hug.

Still breathing hard, Reggie shook his head. "Hey, I'm sorry you had to deal with that. Are you okay?"

"Yeah. Yeah, I'm fine." She mustered a smile, putting her hand over his. "Thanks for sticking up for me."

A strange look passed over the guy's face. "Of course. That's what friends are for, right?"

It had been harder to look Reggie in the eye after that; and her encounters with the rest of her potential suspects hadn't left her feeling any better about eventually facing one of them in a no-holds-barred fight to the death. She would barely even call Cheryl Blossom a friend—and certainly not a close one—but the redheaded girl had surprised Betty, too.

Not long after the incident with the Midville guy, Betty had been singing and laughing with some of the other cheerleaders, and Cheryl had approached them.

"Betty. I'm trying to be understanding, because clearly you're going through something tonight, but your voice is giving me a migraine." Smiling sweetly, the girl added, "Would you mind putting a cork in it?"

"CHERYL!" Betty squealed instead, lunging forward for a hug—but Cheryl stopped her with a stiff arm.

"I don't do hugs." Then, pointing at the cup in Betty's hand, she pursed her lips. "What number is this for you?"

Betty screwed up her face and thought. "Uh . . . I don't know. Three? Four?"

"Okayyy . . ." Pursing her lips, Cheryl pried the drink out of the blonde's hand and passed it to one of the other girls—without asking. "You need to pace yourself, Cooper. You're not some knuckle-dragging frat boy at his first Mardi Gras; you are a River Vixen, and a lady does not drink until she pukes."

"Don't be such a portypot, Blossom," Betty groused in return—but then she froze, eyes going wide. Clapping a hand on Cheryl's shoulder, she made a tremendously disgusting urp noise, and her shoulders hunched.

"Ohmygosh." Cheryl's face went pale. "Are you going to puke? Are you going to puke right now?" When, in response, Betty dropped to all fours on the ground and started to gag, the redhead began barking orders to the other girls. "Maria, go get her some water. Veronica, look for snacks, preferably something with carbs. Lisa, stop playing that song, or I swear I will stuff your phone sideways down your throat, so help me!"

Then she got down next to Betty, stroking her back soothingly, holding the girl's ponytail out of the way while the blonde belched and spit into the grass.

When the episode was over, Betty straightened up again, offering a weak smile. "Thanks, Cheryl."

"Don't mention it." The girl shifted uncomfortably. "You'd have done the same thing for me, right? Team spirit, and . . . you know, all that stuff."

This time, when Betty wrapped her arms around Cheryl, the cheer team captain didn't resist; in fact, after a moment, she embraced the blond girl back.

Happily, Betty mumbled in her ear, "See? You do do hugs!"

"And if you tell anyone," Cheryl muttered back through her teeth, "I'll drown you right here in the river."

Moose Mason was probably the most outwardly intimidating guy at Riverdale High, pretty much built like a werewolf already, with his broad shoulders and towering stature. He was known to have a short fuse, too, and had picked plenty of fights at school over the years. However, even he turned out to have a softer side.

At one point in the evening, Betty had been chasing a firefly— possibly one of the last of the season—over an uneven stretch of earth close to the trees, and she'd tripped while passing a group of guys from Riverdale. For one horrible moment, she'd been completely out of control and headed for a hard landing . . . but she never touched the ground. A pair of huge hands had snatched her right out of the air, swinging her around and lifting her up.

"Whoops!" Moose exclaimed, effortlessly adjusting her body weight in his arms, his biceps straining against the sleeves of his T-shirt. It was definitely not warm enough for a T-shirt, but Betty *wasn't going to complain too much.* "Be careful, Betty, it's kinda dangerous over here."

"Now you tell me," she rejoined, wrapping her arms around his neck and gazing down at the faraway ground. "I think I dropped my libation."

"That's okay, we'll just get you another." Moose grinned at her, and then he spun around, carrying her toward the little makeshift drink station that had been set up on the flats. All the way there, he asked her a series of concerned questions, making sure she hadn't hurt herself, and only when they reached their destination did he finally set her down, light as a feather. "No more chasing fireflies, okay? I might not be around to save you next time."

"I promise," Betty said, and she blew him a kiss before he ambled away to find his friends again.

She'd barely gotten to see Bingo Wilkin at all, but he'd been kind and sweet when she'd stumbled across him and Jughead by the river. He'd taken her drink away—which, honestly, had been the right thing to do—and he'd made sure she had a safe ride home.

And then there was Jughead himself. They'd known each other since kindergarten, and he'd always been shy, kind, and generous—with everything except his French fries. He'd never picked a fight in his life, rarely had a bad word to say about anyone . . . He was a sweetheart. How could she possibly separate all of that from the beast inside, if he turned out to be her quarry?

Was she really ready to kill one of her friends?

The car came to a stop and Betty blinked, startled out of her reverie, surprised to see that they were at the curb outside her house. Yawning, she worked the kinks out of her neck. "Thanks for driving me, Juggie. You're my hero."

"Can I ask you a weird question?" he blurted, staring out the windshield at the moon. His fingers flexed anxiously, still wrapped around the wheel. "What if you did something . . . bad—really bad—but you couldn't remember ever doing it? Does it still count against you?"

"That depends on what you mean, I guess," Betty murmured, her hand frozen on the buckle of her seat belt. "Legally, it's kind of a gray area. Like, if you snap and do something drastic, the consequences are usually lighter than if the crime is premeditated. But morally?" She studied his profile carefully, his tangle of dark hair, the row of points that crowned his trusty hat. "If you're not in control of your actions, then . . . well, maybe that's kind of a gray area, too."

"Oh." He let out a breath, his shoulders dropping. Clearly, it wasn't what he'd hoped to hear.

"Can I ask one?" Betty twisted the ring on her middle finger, its opal setting giving a shimmer when it caught the light. "What if you had to do something bad, to make a choice you weren't sure you could live with, in order to stop someone else from doing something even worse?"

After a long moment of silence, Jughead gave a hollow laugh. "I don't like this game anymore. Let's play astronauts instead."

In spite of herself, Betty giggled. Once upon a time, they *had* played astronauts together, turning her backyard into the universe and exploring its farthest reaches. While she battled aliens and conquered other planets, Jughead adopted martian orphans and learned how to grow flowers in space. Her laugh ebbed away as the memory finally tugged at something sad in her heart, and she leaned across the center console, squeezing the boy's hand and pressing her lips to his cheek. "Thanks for driving me home, Juggie."

They got out, and Jughead waited by the car while Betty made her way up the front walk, clutching her keys so tightly the metal bit into her fingers. When she unlocked the door, she smiled and sketched a wave good-bye, which he returned before starting along the street for his short walk home.

As soon as she was inside, the door shut safely behind her, Betty's smile dissolved. Her lips still tingled from the heat that had pulsed off Jughead's skin, a feverish temperature that hadn't matched his pale, drawn complexion. It was the same heat she'd felt when running her hands through Bingo Wilkin's hair, and when she'd caressed his face and cooed about his music.

All night long, she'd danced around that party with a bright, loose smile and a slushy mouth, playing the part of the drunk party girl to the hilt. The louder and goofier she acted, the clumsier and overly intimate, the more people dropped their guards. They had tolerated her hanging on them, touching them, jumping into their arms . . . but she hadn't swallowed a single drop of alcohol the whole time she was there. She was stone-cold sober.

Slipping the opal ring off her finger, she flicked open the setting, the stone swinging on a tiny hinge to reveal a digital display underneath. One of Aunt Elena's countless useful gadgets, it was a camouflaged thermometer, with a tiny sensor built into the band. Incredibly precise, it could read a person's body temperature after only a second or two of direct contact with their skin. Like when she'd touched Jughead's hand in the car as she'd leaned over the seat to kiss him good-bye.

The display read 102—the exact same number she'd picked up from Bingo Wilkin. It was six degrees above a human being's normal resting temperature, and only one or two degrees away from the kind of fever that would require a trip to the ER . . . but it was the average temperature of a canine. Or of a lycanthrope, whose inner beast was rising to the call of the full moon.

Mounting the stairs with heavy feet, Betty went into her bedroom and shut the door. Drawing a sturdy wooden box out from under her bed, she unlocked it and opened the lid to reveal a gleaming revolver resting on a cushion of pink satin. After a quick but careful inspection, she took a second box from her nightstand and began to load the pistol's cylinder with custom-made silver bullets, her heart sinking into her stomach.

They were far too old to play astronauts now.

ELEVEN

AS SOON AS HE ROUNDED the corner, Jughead broke into a run. Whatever the hell was wrong with Bingo, he'd been dead right when he made that comment about his cousin's skin not fitting right. It was like it was getting smaller by the minute, strangling him, and his blood practically crackled with heat. His limbs twitching, he picked up speed, trying to burn off the strange energy that coursed through him; but the faster he went, the worse the sensation got.

His stomach cramped hard, and he stumbled a little in the road, slowing down. Already his face dripped with sweat, his jacket turning into a furnace, and he wriggled it off his shoulders as he gulped down some chilly air. The clouds parted overhead, dark curtains sliding open to reveal a moon so bright it hurt his eyes, and another pang sheared through his stomach and nearly brought him to his knees. He hadn't eaten all day—again—and the hunger was finally catching up to him.

At a loping gate, he reached an intersection and headed west, some inner voice directing him, whispering instructions he couldn't help but obey. *"Because the full moon is up, and your instincts kicked in"*—that's what Bingo had said. Wasn't it? Suddenly it was hard to remember. It couldn't have happened even a full hour ago, and yet it felt like it had been three months since Reggie's stupid party, everything since then a loud blur slowly crushing together in his mind.

The wind shifted just then, a scent reaching him on the night air, and Jughead's stomach rumbled plaintively. He almost groaned, it smelled so good. Unable to resist, he turned into the wind and broke into a gallop, the heavenly aroma making his mouth water to the point that drool spilled over his chin. Jogging through backyards and across a playground, he emerged on a lonely side street facing the back of the Chock'Lit Shoppe.

It was late, the neon signage turned off for the night—but the smell that had pulled him all the way from Betty Cooper's neighborhood was coming from an open garbage bin on the squalid blacktop behind the diner. His hands trembling, his vision tunneling on the large, squat dumpster, Jughead stumbled closer and peered inside. A pile of raw hamburger, pink and glistening in the moonlight, peeked out from a nest of wax paper. It gave off the faintest stench of rot, but the boy couldn't help himself; reaching out, he scooped some up and shoveled it straight into his mouth.

It tasted so good his knees buckled and he crooned out loud, the sound thick and strangely inhuman. The meat was so soft he didn't even need to chew, one handful after another sliding greedily down his throat until all of it was gone. And yet he was still hungry. His stomach flexed and growled, refusing to be satisfied, and Jughead was dizzy with the need for more. *More.*

His arms and legs were stiff as he staggered around the side of the building, the muscles cramping and releasing rhythmically, a dull pain throbbing to life in his jaw. The moon seemed to pulse, its light sliding wildly across the glass windows of the Chock'Lit Shoppe, the parking lot unsteady beneath his feet. The door to the restaurant was locked when he tried the handle—and somewhere, lost in the buzz that filled his mind, was the memory that it was closed for the night. But Jughead was starving now, and there was food inside. *He could smell it.*

Pounding the glass, he gritted his teeth against a fierce pain that swelled inside of him, every inch of his skin vibrating. It seemed to take forever before a tall figure appeared beyond the slick of blazing moonlight that covered the door, coming closer, sliding open the dead bolt.

"Jughead?" Pop Tate's thick eyebrows angled upward in surprise, his irritation poorly disguised. "What are you doing here, for cryin' out loud—do you have any idea what time it is? We're closed!"

Jughead struggled to speak, but his throat was all wrong, and his lungs were on fire. Yanking hard at the neck of his shirt, the fabric tearing like tissue paper, he growled out the only word he could manage. *"Hungryyyy . . ."*

Pop Tate's expression went from annoyed to alarmed in a heartbeat when Jughead cocked his head to the side with a sickening *crack*, and the man's face turned gray. "Y-your *eyes.* What the hell—*what are you?*"

He tried to slam the door shut, but Jughead caught the edge of the frame with a hand that didn't look anything like his own. It was huge, the nails thick and black, and hair sprouted from his knuckles. Pop Tate pushed harder, but the boy barely felt any resistance, more fabric splitting across his shoulders as the bones stretched and the muscles bulged.

With a shove, he forced his way inside at last, the door crashing open and sending Pop Tate flying across the slippery tile. The man collided with the diner's old-fashioned jukebox and sprawled to the floor, rolling onto his back with wide, frantic eyes. A song started to play, something jaunty and inappropriate, and it disguised the sound of more bones cracking as Jughead's knees snapped the wrong way.

He barely felt it, too focused on the escalating pressure in his jaw, his face twisting into a brand-new shape as he lumbered forward. *"It hurts worse if you resist."* Bingo's words echoed dimly in his mind—but he could barely even remember what they meant, now. All he could think about was the stretch in his shoulders, the throbbing of hot blood in his veins, and the bottomless chasm in his stomach. He was drooling again as he smelled the cowering man's primal fear in the air. The allure of it was indescribable.

"HUNGRYYYY . . ."

When he finally lunged, his teeth sank deep into helpless flesh, and blood spattered the rollicking jukebox. Jughead always enjoyed eating at the Chock'Lit Shoppe.

PART TWO:
THE BEAST MUST DIE

ONE MONTH LATER

TWELVE

WHEN THE MUSIC STARTED playing, Archie took a breath to center himself, and then he charged out of the shadows at full speed. With a graceful leap, he cleared the first obstacle, landing in a tuck and rolling up to his knees. Drawing matching pistols from twin shoulder holsters, he fired on the row of targets that sprang up on either side, leaving smears of black paint across four out of six. Then, jumping to his feet, he dove into the next portion of the course.

In the weeks since Pop Tate was eviscerated at the Chock'Lit Shoppe, Archie had spent almost every evening at Elena Cooper's gym, pushing himself to the limit. He'd learned to shoot, picked up sparring techniques, and studied every book the woman had on the history and lore of werewolves. The full moon was almost upon them again, and

Archie wanted to be ready. There was still a ways to go before he could stand toe-to-toe with either of the Cooper women—let alone an actual monster—but the progress he'd made in the past month was impressive enough that even Betty's hard-to-please aunt had been forced to acknowledge it.

"You're slowing down, Coppertop!" Elena taunted from the sidelines, a stopwatch in her hand. "Every time you try a trick you're not ready for, you lose a second off your best time. Keep your head in the game."

Archie set his jaw and simply pushed harder, lunging into the elevated portion of the course with a determined growl. A network of bungees suspended narrow, untrustworthy footholds several feet off the ground, while targets spun at unpredictable intervals—one side showing the face of a beast, and the other an innocent bystander. It was a challenge they'd designed together, the three of them, and besting it demanded balance and precision.

His foot slipped from the third foothold, and Archie nearly plummeted to the ground, losing one of his pistols and just barely catching on to a bungee in time. Swinging by one hand, the floor ten feet below, he felt every lost second as he struggled back up onto the course. Taking out the targets with his remaining weapon, he tried to make up for lost time; and when he reached the end, he was breathing hard and dripping sweat.

"Not bad, kid." Elena tossed him a towel and a bottle of water, both of which he gratefully accepted. "You're making me less sorry I agreed to train you."

"It wasn't good enough." His hands on his knees, Archie shut his eyes. "I almost fell."

"No, you *did* fall," Elena corrected him. "You were being reckless, you lost control, and you screwed up. But you also caught yourself, got back into the course, and finished anyway." It was as close to praise as she ever got, and he looked up in time to catch a smile flicker across her face. Pride swelled in his chest, and he struggled to keep from showing how delighted he was. She *hated* when he looked delighted. "You want to do more than you're capable of right now—that's called ambition. It's not a bad thing."

"He also shot an old lady," a third voice called out from the far side of the course. Jumping down from the ladder she'd used to retrieve the elevated targets, Betty held one of them up. Its front displayed a snarling werewolf, while the back side showed the smiling face of an elderly woman—with black paint splattered right between her eyes. "I mean, with pretty good aim, but . . . still."

When he first told Betty he would be training under her aunt, the girl had been worried—not because she doubted him, necessarily, but because she knew what fighting monsters entailed, and he . . . didn't. But he'd worked hard to prove his worthiness, to both the Cooper women, and he was pretty sure he'd succeeded. And Betty had eventually been forced to admit that it was nice to have someone to spar with besides Elena, someone to gripe with *about* Elena, and someone with whom to strategize their dire mission.

Even so, it was hard to forget how much less experience and practice he had than someone he'd only ever thought of—until very recently—as just the Girl Next Door.

"Sorry." Archie shook his head, tossing the sweaty towel onto the floor. "I guess I lost my concentration."

"Don't be too sorry." Elena grabbed the target from Betty when the girl approached, trading her for a hip holster and a freshly loaded paint pistol. It was her turn on the course next. "For all you know, our sweet old grandma here turns into your worst nightmare under the full moon. 'What big eyes you've got,' etcetera. Sometimes casualties are inevitable," the woman added with a grave expression. "You need to be ready for that. Sometimes you have to kill to be kind."

"I don't want to kill innocent people." Archie frowned, crossing his arms. "Isn't that the whole point of all this? To *save* those people?"

"Why don't you ask Terry Tate what the point is?" Elena shot back, her eyes narrowing. "Why don't you ask our cousin Jacob—if he shows up tomorrow."

Jabbing her finger into Archie's chest, she snapped, "You

don't know what innocent looks like, Andrews. None of us do. *That's* the point."

"Ask Terry Tate." Automatically, Archie shot a glance at Betty, who had her own eyes carefully averted as she checked the straps of her holster. It had been a month, and yet they still hadn't spoken about what had happened the night of Reggie's party—the night Pop Tate was torn to pieces inside the Chock'Lit Shoppe. There'd been no new victims since then, and the whole town of Riverdale had been on a weird sort of tenterhooks ever since.

Like Betty, Archie knew the beast was still out there, lying dormant until the lunar cycle completed and the moon returned to full—twenty-four hours from now.

"Here's some breaking news I really shouldn't have to share with you," Elena went on, her tone sharp enough to cut through the bars of Jacob Cooper's cell. "Whoever this beast is? They're walking around right now, petting kittens and smiling at cashiers, because they *are* innocent twenty-some-odd days out of the month. The killer could be your worst enemy or your best friend, and either way you've still got to be ready to pull the trigger."

Archie flinched at the not-quite-hypothetical mention of his best friend, and Betty glared at her aunt. "Elena."

"No, this is asinine!" The woman turned her head sharply, her dark hair swinging, and the three shiny scars on her cheek glistened in the light. "He already knows the Jones kid is on the table as a possible player, here. He needs to be ready for that—*you* should have been getting him ready for that for the past month."

"It's not Jughead!" Archie returned angrily. "I've known him forever, and you didn't see how messed up he was after Pop Tate died, okay? He's *still* messed up about it! You don't know what you're talking about."

"Betty." Elena turned on her niece, her eyes flashing. "Tomorrow is the first night of the full moon—again. You need to tell him already."

Silence filled the vast warehouse, dense and ominous, and the back of Archie's neck prickled. "Tell me what? What is she talking about, Betts?"

Betty gave her aunt a murderous glare, but her shoulders sagged in defeat, and she let out a breath. "Archie, I've been doing a little investigating on my own this past month, and . . . and I learned some things you need to know."

"Okay." Only the way she said it made it sound the exact opposite of *okay*.

"When the full moon rises, even before they begin their transformation, a lycanthrope's body heat starts to rise—"

"I know all this," Archie interrupted her impatiently. "It was, like, the first thing I read about when I started going through Elena's library."

"Juggie had a temperature of 102 the night of the party by the Wesley Road bridge." She cut right to the chase. "I was checking people all night long, and he was one of only two who weren't squarely in the normal range."

"So he had a fever—big deal!" Archie tossed a hand out. "And before you get into it, because I can see what you're thinking, it kind of explains everything. He fainted at school; he didn't have an appetite; he was totally out of it . . . he was sick. Case closed."

"The Chock'Lit Shoppe is only a twenty-minute walk from our neighborhood," Betty replied quietly, "and according to the authorities, Pop Tate died within thirty minutes or so of when Juggie left my house that night."

"That doesn't prove anything." Archie spoke through his teeth, but fear sparkled up into his chest just the same. "It's not like the town's that big. Everybody in the Riverdale High school district probably lives about a twenty- or thirty-minute walk from the Chock'Lit Shoppe!"

"Yes, but . . . Reggie and Moose were still at the party when Pop Tate was attacked—there were dozens of witnesses. And the Blossoms were at a gala event the night Miss Grundy died." Betty's voice got smaller. "Look, Archie, I'm sorry—"

"All of them?" he challenged. "*All* the Blossoms? I mean, do you even know how big their family is?"

"Actually, yes. I told you we keep records about that stuff."

"And what about Moose's parents? Or Reggie's?" Archie barreled ahead, trying not to sound as panicked as he was starting to feel. "They all have families. It could be somebody's 'sweet old grandma,' right, Elena?"

He knew bringing Betty's aunt back into the argument was a bad move the second the words came out of his mouth, and the woman confirmed this notion immediately. Blunt as a sledgehammer, she said, "Dilton Doiley, Geraldine Grundy, Terry Tate . . . the only thing that connects those three victims is the kids from your high school. Werewolves may be clever, but they're still beasts, and by instinct they hunt familiar territory—often even familiar scents."

"What about the campers?" He was losing ground faster than a beach at high tide. "I still don't even know any of their names! They were the first ones to die, but none of them are connected to Jughead at all—we'd have found out by now if they were." Nervous heat crawled like a rash over his neck, and he couldn't help scratching at it, fear gobbling up his confidence from the inside out. He couldn't accept what they were implying about Jughead. He *wouldn't*. "So that's a huge, JumboTron-sized hole in your theory. Explain that!"

Elena didn't even blink. "Those woods are still familiar territory to anyone who grew up around here, so the campers could simply have been victims of convenience. I was prepared to accept Doiley as a victim of convenience, too, until the rest of the deaths established a different pattern. There was nothing *convenient* about targeting the Grundy woman. The beast had to break into the school from the roof, and then somehow it managed to kill her in her own classroom with the door locked." She folded her arms across her chest. "He broke it down *from the inside* in order to get out once she was dead."

"None of that proves it was Jughead!" Archie finally shouted, his voice embarrassingly unsteady. "You can't even prove the werewolf is a 'he'—you're just guessing!"

"I hate to break it to you, Coppertop, but this isn't exactly a court of law." She gave him a look that could have knocked a bird out of the sky. "I don't need to 'prove' anything, and we don't have time to just sit around, waiting for your friend to confess!" Snatching up Archie's target again, the elderly lady smiling through the blast of black paint, Elena shoved it under his nose. "You want to know why you screwed up tonight? It's because you're still thinking of your targets as either monsters or people, instead of as *objectives*. Even if you take out some old bag by accident, as long as you stop the wolf, you've saved her entire community. Call it a fair trade, and stop panicking about what will happen if you make a mistake." She threw the paint-smeared placard at his feet.

"If I were the one calling the shots here? Your pal Forsythe would have been dealt with already."

"But you're *not* the one calling the shots," Betty interrupted, her voice filled with steel, and they both glanced over at her. "I am. This is *my* mission, Aunt Elena, and I get to decide what collateral damage is acceptable."

Drawing herself up to her full height, the girl stated, "I don't want any innocent lives lost—and that includes Jughead, if he's not the one who's killing these people."

"Having a soft heart is a great quality for a nanny or a veterinarian, but not a werewolf hunter." Elena let out a disappointed sigh. "You need to toughen up, too, Elizabeth. I know this Jones kid is your friend, but people are going to die if you're not willing to make the hard choices when the chips are down."

"It's *my* mission, and *I* decide when the chips are down," Betty repeated, just as strongly as before, and Archie's eyebrows inched up a little. "I'm not killing one of my oldest friends because he *might* be responsible; I need to know for sure."

Elena flung her hands up in resignation, and Archie turned to Betty. Maybe she wasn't on his side, exactly, but at least she didn't *want* to kill Jughead. Besides, something she'd mentioned earlier was still ringing in his ears—still giving him a tiny glimmer of hope. "Who's the other person? You said there were two people at the party with high temperatures."

"It was Juggie's cousin Bingo." Betty shifted her weight uncomfortably. "He left the party just a little bit before we did that night, and nobody seems to know where he went. As far as I can tell, he and Juggie are the only two suspects we've got who don't have alibis for any of the killings."

"Okay, so maybe it's him." For the first time since this conversation started, Archie felt something like relief. "I mean, what do we even know about the guy? He's got were-wolf genes and he shows up at our parties uninvited? He's *way* more likely to be a people-eating monster than Jughead! Jug feels guilty swatting mosquitoes."

"Wilkin lives in Midville," Elena pointed out, "and Midville doesn't have a werewolf problem. Riverdale does. Not to mention the fact that he's not connected to any of the victims."

"The campsite was between Riverdale and Midville," Archie pointed out in return, "and Bingo's not exactly a stranger around here. He's spent enough time with Jug and the rest of us to know what our lives are like, who our teachers are. All those books you made me read talk about werewolves being super smart, right? So maybe he's killing people over here in order to divert suspicion."

"And maybe the simplest answer is the right one, and your

best bud is eating his way through your social circle." Elena put her hands on her hips. "Or maybe it's both of them together. Either way, you've got about twenty hours before the full moon rises again and people start to die; so if I were you, I'd stop bickering about who the beast is and focus on how you're going to kill it."

With that, she turned around and stalked off, heading for a pile of fresh targets so she could reset the obstacle course. The music kicked in again a beat later, a hard-driving guitar riff and a lead singer who sounded like he was being strangled with piano wire. Wordlessly, Betty spun on her heel and hastened after her aunt—leaving Archie alone with a growing sense of anxious foreboding. Rubbing his neck, he looked down at his feet, where the face of that unfortunate old woman grinned madly back up at him.

Jughead was the one they might be hunting . . . so why did Archie feel like he was the one wearing the target?

THIRTEEN

THREE WEEKS EARLIER, LESS THAN seven days *after the gruesome remains of what had once been Pop Tate were found inside the Chock'Lit Shoppe, Jughead was hiding in a bathroom stall at Riverdale High waiting for the hallways to empty. The school had finally reopened that morning, and his mom had refused to fall for his too-sick-to-go-to-class act. He would rather have been anywhere else, but if he skipped and she found out, Mrs. Jones would swiftly replace the Riverdale Ripper as the scariest creature in town.*

The Riverdale Ripper.

He *was* the Riverdale Ripper. *A deranged laugh bubbled up his throat, but when he coughed it out, it turned into a whimper. He felt like he was losing his mind, and he didn't know what to do anymore. He had killed Pop Tate.*

He had eaten *Pop Tate.*

A flat tone sounded, signaling the one-minute warning, and feet began stampeding in the halls outside. He waited until there were only thirty seconds left—just enough time to get to class, where he could sit with his head down and not talk to anyone. All week long he'd avoided his friends, ignoring their texts and pretending to be asleep if they stopped by his house; and today, he'd skulked around corners, ducking through doorways, and acted like he didn't know his own name when Archie shouted it from the other end of the corridor. He couldn't face them. He could barely face himself.

Peeking out of the bathroom, making sure the coast was clear, he dashed down the hallway. There were still a few people hanging out by their lockers, but no one he knew well enough to talk to, and Jughead thanked whichever last one of his lucky stars was still functioning for that. He barreled around a corner, thirty feet from his classroom door—across from Grundy's, which was now closed and locked for the foreseeable future—and ran straight into someone wearing a letterman's jacket and heading in the opposite direction.

"Whoa! Sorry, I—Jughead?"

Even before his brain caught up with his eyes, Jughead froze solid, a bottomless pit opening up beneath his hopes as he found himself face-to-face with Archie Andrews for the first time since he'd learned the truth about himself . . . and what he'd done. For a long moment, he couldn't remember how to speak. He wanted to shove past the guy and flee—maybe just head right for the door and keep running until he hit the state line. The funny-because-it-was-sad fact of the matter, though, was that if he ducked Archie now, after ghosting him for a week, it would only invite questions he couldn't answer. And he had enough of those already.

"Hey, man, where've you been all week?" Archie asked when Jughead didn't say anything. There was something in his tone that sounded an awful lot like suspicion, and the hallway shrank a little around them. "I've been texting you."

"Yeah, sorry, I—" Jughead's throat closed in a sudden panic, and it took him a beat to find his voice again. "I haven't been feeling well. It's . . . the past few days have been kinda rough."

"Because of Pop?" Archie supplied, his tone almost hopeful. The final bell rang out, but the guy didn't even blink—like the question was some kind of a test. He just kept staring through the unbearably awkward silence that followed, until he finally added, "I . . . can't believe he's dead, you know? I can't believe the Chock'Lit Shoppe is closed."

"Yeah, me neither." Jughead gripped the straps of his backpack so tight his knuckles cracked. Some events from the night he had dropped Betty off at home remained a peaceful blur . . . but other parts were rapidly coming back to him: gruesome images, fragments of something so unspeakably hideous that they turned his blood to ice and made him sick. And this time Jughead was certain they weren't from a dream.

"You can always call me to talk," Archie blurted, looking his friend in the chest, his cheeks turning pink. "If something's . . . going on, or whatever? You . . . you always think you need to deal with the heavy stuff by yourself, but you don't."

It could have been a friendly gesture, but caught in the grips of spiraling paranoia, Jughead saw only another test—a clumsy invitation to confess his crimes. His doubts must have been written plainly on his face, because Archie stammered as he rushed on. "Y-you spent more time at the Chock'Lit Shoppe than any of us. And sometimes it just helps to share, you know?"

"Sometimes it doesn't," Jughead returned, way more emphatically than he meant to. But he couldn't share this, and Archie couldn't help him. No one could. "I really need to get to class."

He didn't wait for a counterargument, just stepped around his friend and raced for the door, but behind him, he heard Archie say, "Even if you don't want to talk about it, we can still hang out. I . . . I'm worried about you, Jug."

Jughead didn't answer. How could he explain that he was worried about himself, too?

♛♛♛

After his disastrous run-in with Archie, Jughead had made a point of trying to act as normal as possible around his friends, hiding his discomfort as best he could whenever the topic of conversation inevitably turned to the Riverdale Ripper. But now, mere hours before sundown on the night of another full moon, he stood at the back of Moore's Hardware Supply, his stomach tied in the kind of knots that Boy Scouts win merit badges for.

There were still more than three hours to go until sunset, but already he could feel the itch beneath his skin, the heat climbing in his blood. His vision wobbled as his eyes filled with tears, and he blinked the moisture away with a shaky breath. In front of him was a selection of heavy-duty chains, the largest and sturdiest with links as big around as his fingers, and he was running out of time to get up the courage to make his purchase.

This was supposed to be the easy part. No one knew why he was there, and he might have a million reasons for buying the kind of chains they use to keep SUVs from rolling off auto-transport trailers. But going through with it—picking out chains, selecting a padlock, going up to pay for them—meant accepting that all of this was real.

There was no turning back now.

Just thinking about the whole situation brought a hysterical laugh to Jughead's lips. A dozen times a day over the past month, the absurdity of it all would hit him again suddenly out of the blue, and he would start to worry that maybe he really was losing his mind. What rational person above the age of ten believed in real, actual monsters? Bingo was just another popular kid with the instincts of a bully, and he'd told this ridiculous lie to get under Jughead's skin—and it had worked.

But then there were the details that had emerged over the past month, reports that had been worded carefully to soften the gruesomeness of the killings that had plagued Riverdale. Massive amounts of flesh missing from the bodies, bones that were scored deep with tooth marks, paw prints tracked all over the crime scenes in the victims' blood . . . it added up to an ugly summary he couldn't argue against. And no matter what lies Bingo had told him the night of Reggie's party, at least one thing had been the indisputable truth: *"It'll come back to you soon, cousin, I promise."*

He'd woken up in his own bed the morning after Pop Tate died, with no recollection of how he'd gotten there. His last memory had been saying good-bye to Betty, watching her head up the walk to her front door, his head spinning a little and his stomach painfully empty. The story that had been splashed all over the local news when he'd gotten up, though, had shaken loose the details of yet another grisly dream—a pile of spoiling meat, a grown man's pitiful screams, the taste of warm, slippery blood coursing down his throat—and Jughead had started to panic.

But, of course, they weren't dreams at all; they were *memories*, and they were quickly joined by others, first in a trickle and then in a flood, complete with taste and sound and texture. The shredding of tent fabric and the terrified shrieks of the campers inside, their eyes bulging in horror. Hunkering down in the mildewy darkness of the old crypt, his heart thudding with anticipation, his stomach growling. Pursuing Miss Grundy along the shadowed hallway of the high school, letting her stay ahead but knowing he could take her down any time he wanted. Pop Tate on his back, the tile floor covered in blood, the man's flesh being torn open by dark claws at the end of thick, inhuman fingers—*his fingers*.

Jughead *was* a real, actual monster. A *werewolf*. And the full moon was due to rise in a matter of hours.

Adrenaline scratched his veins on the inside, his arms and legs jittery and restless, and all day long his stomach had turned at the smell of anything other than raw meat. Grabbing the heaviest, thickest set of chains, and the biggest padlock he could find, Jughead hurried the items to the front of the store. All he could hope for at this point was that these would be strong enough to hold him—that when he transformed, it would keep him from breaking free and taking yet another human life.

When he checked out, the bag was so heavy the muscles in his arms burned as he struggled out the door with it, and the absurdity struck him once again. He could barely lift the chains now, but before the night was over, he'd consider it a lucky miracle if they even slowed him down.

He was halfway across the parking lot when he looked up and froze, the bag slipping from his hand and hitting the pavement with a loud clink. Leaning against Jughead's bicycle, wearing a peacoat and a self-satisfied smirk, was Bingo Wilkin.

"Well, hey there, Forsythe." The boy's tone was benign, almost friendly, but Jughead sensed the threat that hung between them. "Long time, no see."

"Yeah. Long time, no see for a *reason*, Bingo," Jughead snapped, his already rattled nerves fraying just a little bit more. He'd been avoiding his cousin like the plague since the death of Pop Tate—declining his calls and deleting his texts—and he'd even snuck out his bedroom window one afternoon, when Bingo showed up unannounced at the Joneses' house. "Maybe you should learn how to take a hint."

"Maybe I'm not the one who's having trouble facing what's right in front of him," Bingo rejoined mildly. Pushing off the side of the parked bicycle, he sauntered closer, peeking into the bag of chains as Jughead heaved it up off the ground again. "I'd ask what these are for, but I've got a feeling the answer's gonna be really disappointing."

"I know why you came looking for me, but you can just get lost, because I don't want anything to do with you." Jughead pushed around him, heading for his bike, suddenly wishing he'd brought a backpack. How was he going to get these things home?

"Too bad for you that we're linked together by blood,

then, huh?" Bingo asked, following right along behind him. "And all those other things we have in common—"

"We have *nothing* in common!" Jughead snarled, spinning around, his teeth bared and his eyes blazing. Once upon a time, he'd have been thrilled by a comparison to his talented, good-looking cousin—once upon a time, he'd *wanted* to be more like Bingo. He'd never misjudged someone more profoundly, or been so horrified by what traits they actually shared. "I am nothing like you, and I don't want to be, either, okay? You need to get that through your head, and just *leave. Me. Alone.*"

"I'm afraid I can't do that, man." Bingo smiled, calm and casual—but his eyes were colder than the approaching October night. "I tried to tell you last month that we're part of the same pack. You and me? We're bonded together whether you like it or not, *cousin.*"

"I'm not part of anything!" Jughead shouted. He was so loud that a man getting into his car on the other side of the lot looked up with a sharp glance, and the boy lowered his voice. "You're some kind of a psychopath if you actually like being what we are—if you like doing the . . . the *things* we've done." He shuddered all over as terrible images flashed through his mind like an ugly newsreel, his breath catching, bile creeping up the back of his throat. "I never, ever want to see you again, Bingo. Just . . . stay out of my life."

"So you can do . . . what, exactly?" his cousin taunted, falling right into step with him again as Jughead made for his bike. "Chain yourself up like someone's pet schnauzer? Mope and pout and cry like some sad little loser because a twist of fate made you better than ninety-nine percent of the rest of humanity?"

"Better?" Jughead wheeled on Bingo again, his hands clenched into fists. "You call this better? We're *monsters*! People are dead because of us—we killed people and ruined lives, and . . . and don't you even care about that?"

"No. I don't." Bingo's expression remained serene and untroubled. "People die every day; it's not like your buddy Dilton is special just because he punched his ticket last month instead of next month."

"Are you kidding me?" Jughead was appalled. "He didn't 'punch his ticket'—*we* did!"

"And you think that if I feel bad enough about it that it would make a difference to someone?" Bingo asked with genuine puzzlement. "He could've died choking on a piece of candy, or crossing the street without looking both ways . . . It's not like he was gonna live forever if we hadn't intervened, or something."

"That's not the point!"

"It *is* the point. It's the only point." Bingo stepped closer, until Jughead could smell his expensive cologne. "Humans might make art and do math and walk around on two feet, but they're still animals, and this is how the animal kingdom works: The weak die so the strong can survive. That's just a fact." Reaching over, he plucked a piece of lint off his cousin's jacket, and Jughead lurched back reflexively. "People love to act all sad when they see lions take down a gazelle on one of those nature shows, but guess what? If the gazelles all get away, then the lion cubs starve to death. Which one's better? Which one doesn't deserve to die?"

"You're twisting this all around!" Jughead jabbed an accusing finger at him. "You're making it sound like it was them or us, like we didn't have a choice, and that's not . . ." His windpipe closed, choking off the rest of a statement he wasn't even sure how to finish anyway—because if he'd had a choice, none of this would have happened. Unable to muster his full voice, he whispered, "I don't want to kill anyone else, Bingo. I don't want to be a monster."

"You keep saying that word, but we're not 'monsters,' man. We're *titans*." Bingo's eyes lit up—literally—a bright, golden glow dancing in his pupils. "We're the top of the food chain! How many times have you told me how much you hate this chemical toilet of a town, anyway? All these pathetic, stuck-up Riverdale sheep with their boring lives, always following each other around, trying to be the first one to do what everybody else is doing. Don't act like you don't think you're better than them—like you don't *know* it."

"I . . . I don't," he insisted weakly, but he didn't even sound convincing to his own ears. He'd spent his whole life being teased and excluded by most of the kids he went to school with, and he'd figured out early on that he just didn't care—that it actually spoke highly of his character that he didn't fit in with the popular crowd. Everything about them was generic and cruel and fake, and he absolutely considered himself better than that.

The only people he knew who had offered him nothing but genuine friendship, had been nice to him without expecting anything in return, were Archie Andrews and Betty Cooper. The fact was, if a disaster-movie-type scenario happened in Riverdale, Jughead had decided long ago that they were the only ones in town he'd bother to save. But now his life *was* a disaster, and he wasn't sure if he could save anyone—least of all himself.

"This is who you are, Jughead." Bingo's tone was measured and calm. "You can love it or you can hate it, but you can't change it. This world is all about survival of the fittest, man or beast—and you and me? We're the fittest to survive." The light in his eyes grew brighter, and his eyeteeth sharpened as he grinned. "These people are our food *and* our entertainment, and the sooner you accept that the happier you'll be."

"Get away from me." Jughead stepped back, bumping into his bicycle and nearly toppling it over. The wind shifted, scattering crisp brown leaves across the small lot of the hardware store, and the bag of chains hung like an albatross from his straining grip. "Go back to Midville and stay there—or, better yet? Go to hell."

Jughead was on his bike, pedaling away, when Bingo called after him, "Don't worry about that, cousin. We're *both* going to hell."

The wind picked up, tossing the branches of the trees overhead, and the chattering of dried leaves sounded like a chorus of hideous, mocking laughter.

FOURTEEN

WITH THIRTY MINUTES TO GO until sunset, Archie was lying on his bed with his headphones on, staring at the ceiling. He had the volume as loud as he could stand it, because otherwise he was afraid he'd hear his phone and then he'd have to pick it up. Then he'd have to face what he had promised to be part of tonight.

He was being childish and he knew it, but he just didn't want to admit that Jughead could be the Riverdale Ripper. Okay, so the guy *had* been acting a little strange over the past month—but so what? This was *Jughead* they were talking about. He *always* acted strange. He took pride in it. On the other hand, of course, was the fact that Archie had known very well there was a possibility he'd be hunting his best friend when he asked Elena to train him in the first place.

Now the full moon was on its way to claiming the sky,

to working its influence over the werewolf that had been terrorizing the city, and Archie had to decide if he was going to do something about it or not.

Could he live with himself if it turned out the creature he was supposed to hunt was his best friend?

Could he live with himself if it turned out his best friend was killing people and he did nothing to stop it?

Another minute ticked off the clock, and with an agonized growl, Archie ripped the headphones away from his ears. His phone was vibrating madly, like he'd known it would be, and as he snatched it off his nightstand he jerked open the blinds. Betty was watching him from her bedroom window, her own phone pressed to her ear, her expression grim.

"I'm here," Archie snapped into his cell, scowling across the distance between them.

"I can see that." She didn't sound angry, but she didn't exactly sound warm, either. For a moment, he wasn't sure which way this conversation was about to go. But then she added, "Listen . . . I am sorry I didn't tell you earlier about what I'd learned at Reggie's party. Honestly, I just didn't know how. I don't want it to be Juggie, either."

Even as far apart as they were, he could tell when her expression softened, when her posture drooped with regret. Letting out a sigh, Archie glanced down at his feet. "It's bad no matter who it is. And I'm sorry that I freaked out on you like that. This is . . . it's just hard, you know? All I wanted was for your aunt to teach me how to face this so I wouldn't feel so helpless anymore, but now that it's actually go time, now that it's actually *here*—"

"You feel helpless anyway?"

"Yeah. A little." He looked up again. "Even if it's Bingo, it's still someone we know. We still have to go hunting for someone we've hung out with."

Betty sighed before speaking again. "Look, Archie. I really *could* use your help—and, honestly, I was kind of relieved thinking I wouldn't have to do this alone . . . but if the whole thing is too hard for you . . ."

"What about wolfsbane?" he asked suddenly, recalling the night he'd learned about werewolves for the first time—the conversation they'd had in the parking lot of Elena's secret gym. He watched Betty from across the way, trying to study her expression in the glow from her bedside lamp, the clouds behind the Cooper house so thick that the sky was already dark.

Betty's shoulders sagged. "Archie—"

"No, hear me out, okay?" He put up a hand. "I read all those books in your aunt's library, and a bunch of them included rumors about wol—"

"Wolfsbane serving as a cure for lycanthropy?" Betty concluded the statement for him, her tone weary. "I've read all those same books, too, Archie, and there's a reason we still call them 'rumors.' I mean, if a cure actually worked, don't you think we'd have used it by now?" She sighed. "My cousin Jacob hasn't shown up at Elena's gym yet, and he's not answering his phone, either. She might have to drive out to his place in Greendale and start tracking him—she might have to kill him, if things go south. If we could have cured him . . ."

"I'm sorry," Archie answered quietly.

"It sucks," she acknowledged. Then: "It's also part of the job."

She was watching him carefully from her window, and he knew what point she was trying to make—but he wasn't ready to give up yet. "Why would those rumors still be going around if there's nothing to them, though? I mean, can you *prove* there's no way it could work?"

"No one's ever proven that it *can*," Betty countered. "Look, the rumors persist because, since the dawn of time, werewolves who didn't want to be killed by angry villagers had to convince them that a cure existed. The rumors persist because people want to believe them." She switched her phone from one hand to the other. "All we know about wolfsbane for a fact is that it's poisonous—to humans *and* lycanthropes—and that *some* werewolves have had limited success using it in small doses to help inhibit the change. But that doesn't mean—"

"Wait, so it *can* help?" Archie perked up excitedly, even as he watched Betty slap an aggravated hand over her eyes.

"Listen to me, okay? *Some* werewolves have had *limited* success, but it's like homeopathic medicine—we don't know how it works, or even *if* it works. People say it does, but we can't be sure it isn't just a placebo effect."

Archie tried not to look as confused as he felt. "A . . . a what?"

"A placebo is a treatment that doesn't actually do anything, but the patient gets better anyway, because they believe in it. Professionals have documented the effect lots of times—it shows that attitude and psychology are linked to the healing process."

"Wow. That's . . . kind of cool, I guess?"

"I learned that from Dilton," Betty said, leaning against the window frame with a sad look. "Look, Jacob tried wolfsbane the first few months, and all it did was make him sick. And even in the cases where it seems to help, it's only temporary, because eventually the beast wants out. That's its nature, Archie, and they can't fight it."

Turning her gaze out at the night, at the lampposts along the street and the heavy shadows gathering beyond them, she added, "The only guaranteed ways to stop a werewolf are a silver bullet or a blade to the neck. We can't take chances with this. It's always better safe than sorry—especially when lives are at stake."

Archie shuddered all over. He'd spent the last month thinking of the Riverdale Ripper as a creature, like the thing Elena kept caged up at the back of the warehouse—some ravening, dangerous monster. It was one thing to know that the animal hurling itself at those silver-coated bars in a murderous frenzy was a normal human being for twenty-eight days out of every thirty-one, but it was another to have met that person face-to-face. It was another to have grown up with him, learned to read with him, gone to his birthday parties, and listened to him cry over skinned knees and bad dreams. "Betts . . ."

"I'm sorry, Archie, I really am." Her face was tipped down, her expression unreadable, but her voice had pain in it. "I'd change this if I could, but I can't. And if we don't do something to stop the wolf, whoever it is, more people are going to die. We've already lost a friend, a teacher, and Pop Tate . . . who's next? Veronica? Your parents?"

"Okay," Archie said in a hoarse voice—because, rather foolishly, it was the first time he'd even considered that his parents might be at risk. They didn't even know werewolves were real, and they'd probably have him committed if he tried to warn them. But the Ripper was definitely focused on people in Jughead's life, and that included Mr. and Mrs. Andrews . . .

who wouldn't think twice about opening the door for Jug or Bingo. "You're right. Of course you're right. We have to stop this thing, no . . . no matter what."

"Then you're in?"

"On one condition." He licked his lips, looking over at his bed, where he'd tossed the target that Elena had made him take home from the gym the night before. The kindly old woman smiled back at him through the kill-shot splatter of black paint. "I get Jughead."

On the other side of the gulf between their houses, Betty's eyebrows shot up. "Excuse me?"

"There's two of us and two of them, and the easiest way to do this is if we split up," Archie stated. "So you go after Bingo, and I get Jughead."

"No offense," Betty returned lightly, "but are you sure that's a good idea? I mean . . . come on, Archie, you can't tell me you're not emotionally involved here. This isn't the kind of situation where you can afford to hesitate, and if it's Jughead . . ."

"No offense? But he's my best friend, and I'm not gonna let you or anybody else blow his brains out if he sneezes under the full moon, because it's 'better safe than sorry.'"

She drew a breath, and he could tell she was stifling her annoyance. "Okay, but—"

"No buts. That's my condition." He was brusque. "I either

get Jughead, or I sit this out altogether, and you can go after them alone."

There was a long silence as they watched each other from their bedrooms, a standoff as the sun sank lower and lower behind the clouds, and the moon began its arc into the evening sky. For a moment, he wasn't sure what Betty would say. She couldn't watch both targets at once, and she knew it; but Archie wasn't exactly an indispensable assistant, and they both knew that, too. Finally, however, she let out a heavy breath.

"All right, you win. I'll take Bingo; you take Jughead." Her bedroom light went out, plunging her window into darkness, but before she hung up, she added, "But, Archie? If you hesitate and people get killed? It's on you."

FIFTEEN

THE CRIME SCENE TAPE HAD been removed from the old cemetery's gates, but it was still a place only ghouls would enter—especially after a teenager was killed and eaten there. It didn't stop Archie from glancing up the hillside as he drove past, however, his eyes checking among the headstones for ghostly lights or the shape of an inhuman creature searching for its next meal. He tried not to think about what it meant that Dilton's fatal attack had happened only minutes from Jughead's front door. He tried not to think about much of anything.

One of the lampposts was out on Jughead's street, leaving a darkened stretch of curb where Archie parked his car, only a block and a half away from the Joneses' house. It still felt too close. It's not like he had an unmarked vehicle to perform this amateur surveillance in, and every member of his best friend's family would recognize his dented-up four-door if they saw it. Saying a prayer that this night would be the most boring he'd ever spent, Archie reached into his glove compartment for the item Betty had given him only fifteen minutes earlier.

The brushed steel handgun had already been intimidatingly heavy before she'd loaded it with a magazine containing eight silver bullets. Double-checking the safety, she'd presented it grip-first, and all she'd said was, "You know how it works. The bullets aren't easy to come by, so make every shot count."

A block and a half up, just visible beyond the overhang of a neighbor's porch, Jughead's bedroom window was a square of bright light in the gathering gloom. Behind the curtains, a shape moved back and forth—while inside the car, Archie checked and rechecked the gun, his stomach aching with nerves and regret. He'd won his argument with Betty, but now that he'd gotten what he wanted, he wasn't so sure he wanted it anymore. What if he really had to use this thing tonight? What if he had no other choice?

"Please stay home, Jug," he whispered into the quiet privacy of his car, his eyes sliding shut. "Please just . . . stay home."

Clouds still hid the sky, but Betty knew the sun was down and the moon was up by the time she reached the outskirts of Midville, steering off the main road and into the dirt parking lot of a long, low building surrounded by skeletal trees. Music blared from inside, and bleary-eyed men stood outside the front entrance, puffing cigarette smoke into the chilly night air. A neon sign along the roofline spelled out CONEY'S BOWL-O-RAMA.

Lifting her purse from the passenger-side footwell, Betty double-checked the loaded revolver inside before tossing the bag over her shoulder and getting out of the car.

Guilt sat on her chest like something physical, pressing the air from her lungs. She still hadn't told Archie the whole truth. She wasn't sure she'd ever find the words she needed to confess that the night Juggie had taken her home, she'd loaded the very gun she had in her purse now, with plans to go out and track him down again. The part she hadn't told anyone, not even Elena, was that the reality of hunting one of her oldest friends had been so overwhelming that it immobilized her completely. She'd stood there in the street for nearly ten minutes before admitting she couldn't do it and going back inside again.

The next morning, she'd woken up to the news of Pop Tate's death. Another killing on her conscience. Another victim she might have saved if she'd actually confronted the beast when she had the chance. Archie thought he'd pressured her into letting him be the one to go after Jughead tonight, but in truth, Betty was relieved to escape that responsibility.

Inside the bowling alley, the air smelled of stale beer, fresh wax, and musty fabric; pins clattered loudly behind the still-louder music. Past the snack bar and video arcade, a performance space had been set up in a corner near the bar, and there—cast into high relief by hot white lights, and surrounded by a respectably sized crowd—a live band was just finishing a song.

"Hey, everybody," the lead singer murmured into the microphone a moment later. "Thanks for coming out tonight. I'm Bingo, and with me are Samantha on backing vocals and Buddy on drums—and this guy over here, with the bass guitar and the great fashion sense, is Tough Teddy. Together, we're The Bingoes, and this next number goes out to a very special lady—you know who you are."

He could have been talking to anybody, but it felt like he was talking right to *her*—he was that smooth. Betty drifted closer through the crowd as the number started, the bass laying a low, pulsing beat, joined first by the drums, then lead guitar, and finally the vocals. The layering of sound sent a shiver up her spine, the melody slow and haunting, Bingo's voice like honey poured over the chords.

Betty had heard them before but never like this, not so close and personal. They were *good*—and Bingo was an obvious star, his magnetism so strong it pulled attention even from bowlers who were trying to ignore the noise. His eyes closed, the lights picking out the arch of his cheekbones, the pout of his bottom lip—he was almost ethereal—and she shivered again, thinking about the monster that might be lurking behind that angelic face.

"Betty Cooper?" Her own name, spoken in an unexpectedly familiar voice, jarred her out of her thoughts. Turning, she found herself eye to eye with Ethel Muggs. "What are you doing here? Are you a fan of The Bingoes, too?"

"I . . . yeah!" Forcing a bright smile, Betty directed her gaze back to the band, but Bingo's eyes were open, and she was almost certain he was looking at her, so she turned back to Ethel again. "I mean, obviously—they're amazing, right?"

"*So* amazing." Ethel placed both hands over her chest, cartoon hearts practically swimming around her head as she gazed up at the band. "I come to all their shows." An expression of guilty pleasure crossed her face and she confided, "You can't tell anyone but . . . he was talking to me. I'm the 'very special lady' he dedicated the song to!"

Her cheeks flushed with embarrassment, but she smiled ear to ear, and Betty's heart dipped a little. Ethel was pretty and sweet, but she had a tendency to believe the best in everyone, and she wore her vulnerabilities on her sleeve. Meanwhile, Bingo was a known player, with a slate of angry ex-girlfriends that even included a few names from Riverdale High. Trying not to sound skeptical, Betty asked, "Wow, are you serious?"

"Yes." Ethel's tone was indulgent and gleeful. Leaning closer, still shouting to be heard over the music, she confided, "Listen, you seriously have to promise to keep this a secret, but . . . Bingo and I are kind of a 'thing.'"

She giggled, lifting her eyebrows conspiratorially, and Betty tried to look excited. "You mean, like, a boyfriend-girlfriend thing, or . . .?"

"Basically." Ethel seemed to realize how this qualifier sounded, because she hastened to add, "We've been . . . you know, hanging out and stuff for a while, but he doesn't want to make it official yet. There's a record label interested in the band, and their manager says that they'll have a better shot at getting signed if Bingo can tell them he's single."

Betty nodded politely, but her heart dropped all the way to her feet. *He could tell them he's single no matter what*, she wanted to point out; but they weren't close enough friends for her to bring that up. And they were definitely not close enough for her to bring up the fact that Ethel's not-exactly-boyfriend might be a bloodthirsty monster—and that Betty had come to the show with a gun in her purse in case she had to kill him.

Turning back to the band, Betty watched Bingo sing softly into the mic, his eyes closed again, the melody dripping with heartache. Goose bumps made her scalp feel tight. She'd met wolves in sheep's clothing before.

👑👑👑

"Oh, wow, Archiekins," Veronica cooed, squeezing his bicep. "I can't believe all these muscles! You must have been working out, like, *all* year long!"

"I mean, yeah, I hit the gym pretty regularly, I guess." He faked his nonchalance, flexing and stretching so the veins in his forearms would pop out a little bit more. "But that's what you have to do if you want results. Nobody does the hard work for you, right?"

"I admire that so much, you have no idea." Veronica leaned closer, smelling like peaches and vanilla shampoo, and she fluttered her eyelashes. "Actually, I've sort of been mean-ing to tell you that I . . . well, I kind of think you're cute."

Blushing, she bit her lip, and Archie's voice cracked as he asked, "You do?"

"Of course I do, silly." She leaned even closer, her fingers trailing down his chest. "All I've been able to think about all week is what it would be like to—"

Archie's head hit the window and he woke up with a jolt, his eyes snapping open in hazy confusion as the dream dissolved. Momentarily disoriented, he looked around, startled to find himself behind the wheel of his car, his hands and feet freezing as the temperature outside plummeted. Reality came back to him immediately, and he shot a panicked look out the windshield . . . but the light in Jughead's bedroom was still on. His best friend was still at home, and he slumped back into his seat with a sigh of relief.

In the movies, stakeouts always looked cool and exciting, but all he'd done since parking the car was sit on his butt and stare out the window. He'd never been so bored in his entire life. Bouncing up and down in his seat, Archie slapped himself across the face a few times to clear his head. If he fell asleep again and more people got eaten, Betty would kick his butt up around his ears—and he'd kind of deserve it. Coffee was what he really needed, and he reprimanded himself for not thinking to bring some; but then again, coffee would make him need to pee, and if he needed to pee and couldn't go anywhere, he would really be screwed.

And now that he was thinking about it, he kind of had to pee.

Digging through the glove compartment, reaching behind

the gun, he pulled out a tin of breath mints—the kind that were so strong they made your face hurt—and stuffed a couple into his mouth. The fumes hit his sinuses like a blowtorch, and he gasped a little, his eyes tearing up. It was as he was blinking them clear again that Jughead's window went suddenly dark, and Archie stiffened behind the wheel of the car.

It was a Friday night, and way too early for the guy to be going to bed . . . but not too late for him to be going out. Automatically, Archie checked his phone, but his best friend had neither texted nor called. Under his breath, he pleaded, "Please stay home, Jug. Please, please, please stay home."

But as he watched, the bedroom window inched open quietly, and a figure emerged. Reaching for the drainpipe that climbed the side of the house, Jughead swung off the windowsill and vanished from sight. A few seconds later, he was scurrying across the lawn for the sidewalk, wheeling a bicycle beside him that he must have hidden in the side yard. When he cast a furtive glance up the block, Archie ducked down behind the wheel, until his eyes were just barely peeking over the dashboard.

Apparently Jughead didn't notice the car, because with one last look back at the house, he jumped on his bike and pedaled quickly up the street. A backpack was slung over the boy's shoulders, hanging low, and Archie waited until he was almost out of sight before starting the engine and pulling out after him.

Creeping along the curb, keeping the headlights off, Archie's stomach cramped with worry as his worst fears seemed to be coming true right before his eyes.

SIXTEEN

BY THE TIME THE BINGOES' first set was over, Betty knew more about Ethel Muggs than she'd ever wanted to. She also knew more trivia about the band and its members than she'd ever known about werewolves, despite a lifetime of intensive education on the latter. Every lyric from every song seemed to have an important backstory, and Ethel would whisper-shout it as quickly as possible so that she could be ready when Bingo sang the next line, and a new piece of vital information would need to be revealed.

The girl's capacity for recall was actually kind of astounding, and if she could be persuaded to apply those powers elsewhere, Betty figured Ethel could probably complete a full law degree in about two years.

"Okay, gang. We're taking a short break, but we'll be back

on again in a few minutes, so stick around." Bingo smiled into the crowd, his teeth even and white. "If you liked what you've heard so far, our EP is on sale, and you can buy a copy at the bar. And if you're heading home, well, thanks for coming out and please tell your friends about The Bingoes!"

As the lights shifted, coming up in the dingy bar area while going down on the performance space, Ethel turned to Betty with bright pink cheeks. "Ohmygosh I'm so thirsty, I feel like I've been talking your ear off. Do you want a soda, or anything? It's my treat."

"You don't have to do that," Betty said hastily, one eye on Bingo as he put his guitar back in its case. She wasn't exactly expecting him to wolf out in the middle of a show, but she'd heard enough hair-raising stories from Elena to make her aware that nothing was outside the realm of possibility.

"Please, you've been so nice." Ethel took hold of Betty's arm, tugging her toward the bar. "I know how I sound when I get started talking about the band. Midge came to a couple of their gigs with me, but then she stopped because she said she couldn't take it anymore." With another embarrassed giggle, the girl shrugged. "She says I'm obsessed, and . . . well, maybe I am, but can you blame me? I mean, tell me they're not great!"

"They are actually pretty great," Betty had to admit.

"Right? And Bingo is just . . . I mean, *look* at him." Ethel shivered all over. "Anyway, you let me go on and on, so buying you a soda is the least I can do."

Bingo was making his way through the crowd, shaking hands and accepting compliments as he headed to the bar, and so Betty allowed Ethel to tug her in the same direction after all. Still, with a minute frown, she said, "You know, you don't have to apologize for finding something interesting, or for talking to me about it. I'm sorry Midge has a problem with you being a fangirl, or whatever, but, like . . . Midge is dating Moose. I'm not sure she's got a leg to stand on when it comes to criticizing someone else's taste."

It probably wasn't the most diplomatic thing to say, and if Ethel repeated it at school, it was a remark that could easily come back to bite her; but it seemed worth the risk to put the girl at ease. Ethel really was sweet, even if she only seemed capable of holding a conversation about one specific subject.

At the bar, Ethel ordered two sodas, trying and failing not to stare at Bingo the whole time. He was perched on a stool at the other end of the counter, talking and laughing with a group of people Betty didn't recognize—and almost conspicuously avoiding looking over in Ethel's direction. When their glasses hit the table, the two girls clinked them together in a toast, and Betty finally said, "You know, it's a free country. You can go over there and say hi to him if you want to."

"No, I can't," Ethel said quickly, shaking her head. "I mean, he doesn't want me to." Seeing Betty's reaction to this, she hastened to add, "I mean, record labels send undercover scouts to these shows all the time, and he doesn't want to jeopardize a possible deal if they see him with a girl and realize he was lying when he said he was single."

Betty frowned so hard her face almost cramped, and she took a sip of her drink to buy a little time before she replied. "Did *he* tell you that? Because that doesn't sound like a real thing to me. Guys with girlfriends get record deals all the time."

"I know, but it has to do with, like, packaging and marketing and stuff." She made a vague gesture, clearly repeating something she'd been told. "They want to sell him as a heartthrob, and he needs to look like he's . . . you know, available."

"Well, he's sitting with some girls right now," Betty pointed out, "and he doesn't look all that worried about 'availability' issues."

Ethel glanced over and made a face when she saw the trio of blondes who were clustered around Bingo Wilkin. One of them sat a little closer than the others, her hand on the boy's arm, tossing her curly hair with flirtatious regularity. Betty had noticed her during the show, watching the stage, taking pictures, chattering with her friends.

A tiny thread of uncertainty creeping into her voice, Ethel stated, "Those are just fans."

"So are we. Come on." It was a terrible idea, and Betty knew it, but she couldn't keep herself from goading Ethel off her stool and leading her along the bar toward the boy and his "fans." Elena would physically throw her off the planet if she found out Betty had approached a target like this, but it was already too late. "Hey, Bingo, nice job up there. You guys sound great tonight."

"Betty Cooper, what do you know," Bingo greeted her with a delighted smile, as if he hadn't already noticed her. The girls with him gave her a series of suspicious looks, and he explained, "She's from Riverdale—she's friends with my cousin."

"Oh, you're from Riverdale?" One of the blondes winced delicately. "I'm sorry."

Betty couldn't tell if she was being trolled, or if the girl was trying to express sincere condolences for all the murders and stuff, but she decided it didn't matter. "Look who I ran into!"

She presented Ethel with a little nudge, and the girl gave a shy smile and a wave. "H-hey, Bingo."

"Hey . . ." His brow crinkled a little bit, and he tapped the counter a few times like he was thinking hard. "Edith, right? You're another one of Jughead's friends."

"It's . . . it's Ethel. Actually." Her voice faltered, her smile stretching painfully across her teeth, and Bingo gave her a disinterested nod before turning back to the blondes.

Betty felt Ethel tug at her sleeve again, but she ignored the unspoken plea to retreat, anger slowly gathering in her veins. With a viciously bright grin, she leaned forward, interrupting Bingo's conversation and speaking directly to the girl with the curly hair. "Hi, I'm Betty! I'm not sure we've met, have we?"

"No, I don't think so." Politely, the girl obliged, as Betty had predicted she would. "I'm Amber—I'm Bingo's girlfriend."

And there it was. Bingo flinched as the truth was revealed, but Betty's moment of bittersweet triumph turned all the way sour the instant she glanced over at Ethel. Pale and stricken in the overhead light, the girl blinked a few times before blurting, "G-girlfriend? I thought . . . you said . . ."

Betty could see the exact moment the girl realized she'd been lied to—strung along and misled for weeks by a faithless boy who had exploited her rose-tinted trust—and tears spilled from Ethel's eyes a moment before she turned on her heel and rushed out of the bar. Her heart twisting, Betty was about to go after her when she heard one of the blond girls mutter, "What the hell is her problem?"

"I dunno," Bingo answered, sounding utterly bored.

"Maybe she has a crush on me, or something. She's kind of a stalker, but I don't think she's dangerous or anything. My cousin says she's just really weird."

Betty had to count to ten to keep from using his face as a bowling ball, her breath shaking as she drew it in through her nose. As calmly as she could, she said, "Hey, Bingo, make sure you ask the bartender for a towel or something before your next set."

Furrowing his brow, he asked, "Why would I—"

Betty didn't wait for him to finish before she threw the entire contents of her glass right in his face, the ice-cold liquid drenching his hair and soaking into his T-shirt. The blondes gasped and jumped back, and people swiveled around in shock, but Betty gave Amber a tight smile. "He's cheating on you. Probably a lot." Then, slamming her glass back down on the counter, she stormed out.

The temperature had dropped sharply during the show, and her breath clouded the air as she rushed into the parking lot, looking around for signs of her friend. Guilt made her face hot as she remembered Ethel's crushed expression, the look on her face as she'd fled the bar. All Betty had wanted to do was expose Bingo's scumbag lies—to show Ethel that he wasn't worth her devotion—but she'd bungled it. Even if it was better for the truth to be revealed, this had been the wrong way to bring it into the light.

She found the girl at last, huddled under a tree at the edge of the lot, sniffling quietly and wiping her cheeks with her sleeve. Digging into her bag, Betty found a pack of Kleenex and held one out. "Hey. You need this?"

"Thanks," Ethel said dully, accepting the tissue and loudly blowing her nose. Her eyes were swollen, her face blotchy beneath moonlight dulled by cloud cover. "I'm such an idiot."

"You're not—"

"I am." She wrapped her arms around herself, refusing to look up at Betty. "Midge kept telling me that he wasn't really into me—that he was just u-using me. I should've listened to her."

"Don't beat yourself up," Betty said quietly, handing over the whole pack of tissues. "Guys like Bingo . . . they're good at lying, they get a lot of practice. He knew what to say, and you believed him because you're a good person and expected him to be the same way. That makes *him* the idiot, not you."

"And yet I'm the one crying in the parking lot." She tossed a hand out and let it fall. "I'm the one who thought that, for just once, something nice could actually happen to me. You probably think I'm pathetic."

"That's not even—"

"Will you take me home?" Ethel asked abruptly. Misinterpreting Betty's sudden hesitation, she added, "Midge dropped me off, but I can't call her. I can't deal with her saying 'toldja so' right now. Please? You'll have to go right through my neighborhood on the way back to your place anyway."

Casting a glance back at the bowling alley, the light-up sign flickering slightly, Betty chewed on her lip. She had to keep an eye on Bingo, but she couldn't possibly explain why—and at this point, she'd look like the worst kind of friend if she pretended she still wanted to enjoy the rest of the gig after what had just happened. Plus, Ethel wouldn't be so upset if Betty had just *waited*. Bingo might even have to die tonight, in which case all of his lies and secrets could have gone with him, and no one would have had to be hurt at all.

It would take twenty minutes to reach Ethel's place, tops; if she turned right around afterward, Betty could make it back to the Bowl-o-Rama before The Bingoes finished their second set. Letting out a breath, she nodded. "Yeah, of course. I'm parked over here."

♛♛♛

Tailing someone turned out to be yet another thing that looked exciting in the movies but was both difficult and boring in real life. Especially when that someone was on a bike, and you were in a car, and you couldn't let them know you were following them. Even at his fastest, Jughead was too slow for Archie to drive behind him without making his intentions obvious, so he had to hang back far enough that Jug was always just on the edge of vanishing completely from sight. It meant rolling along at an excruciating pace, and worrying constantly that he would lose the guy.

It also meant that he still couldn't turn on his headlights. The roads were almost deserted, which meant no traffic to blend in to, and he had to stay as inconspicuous as possible. It was fine while they were in town, the streets lit in brassy tones by regular lampposts, but when Jughead unexpectedly cycled past the city limits, rushing into the vast darkness of the wooded hills outside Riverdale, Archie began to get nervous.

Clouds still formed a ceiling overhead, slender veins of pale illumination only just beginning to show where the moon bled through, and the otherwise lightless terrain was gloomy and threatening. The world ahead dissolved into shades of black and gray, trees climbing high on either side of the road, and sweat filmed Archie's upper lip as he struggled to see. A truck zoomed by, and the driver shouted obscenities as he swerved around the slow-moving four-door. His heart squeezing painfully, Archie let out a shaky breath, starting to wish he'd never followed Betty out of the Chock'Lit Shoppe that day a month ago.

Jughead pedaled for several miles, the clouds gradually thinning, the road rising and falling as Archie wondered for the millionth time where they were going. At first he'd been afraid they were headed for Midville—that maybe the "both of them did it" theory was true, and the cousins were planning to meet up for a night of unspeakable bloodshed—but this was definitely not the way to the bowling alley where The Bingoes played their regular gig. This was the way to *nowhere*. There was nothing in these woods but—

When it hit him, he almost choked. *There was nothing in these woods but the campsite where a group of college kids had been massacred two months ago.*

Up ahead, the bicycle vanished suddenly around a curve in the road, and more sweat rolled from his temples as he fought the urge to step on the gas. If he lost Jughead at this point, what would he do? And why were they out here? Everything about this felt wrong and ominous, and there were no heartwarming explanations Archie could think of for why his best friend had snuck out of the house in order to take a bike ride into the murder woods under a full moon. Strong-arming Betty into letting him be the one to watch Jughead tonight was very quickly turning into his biggest regret.

When he reached the turn where he'd lost sight of his friend, Archie's panic redoubled, and his fingers tightened on the wheel. Ahead, the road was now a straight shot, and as the clouds slowly peeled back their layers to let more light through, his mouth went completely dry. As far as the eye could see, the blacktop was totally empty. Jughead had vanished.

SEVENTEEN

AT THE ROADSIDE, A SIGN flashed under the Beetle's headlights, promising that it was just three miles to the municipal junkyard—which meant twelve miles to Riverdale, which meant only about fifteen more minutes before Betty could regain peace, quiet, and her mental equilibrium. Thank God.

It turned out that there was only one subject Ethel Muggs enjoyed talking about even more than her comprehensive knowledge of The Bingoes, and that was her newfound, terrifyingly deep hatred of Bingo himself. The girl had barely gotten her seat belt buckled before she hooked up a depressingly awful playlist of sad music and started in on her list of grievances. Betty couldn't exactly blame her, but . . . she also nudged the gas pedal a little closer to the floor, hoping to shave a few more minutes off this ride.

"He never wanted to kiss me where other people could see us, and I didn't even have the guts to ask why, because I was afraid that if I questioned it I'd ruin things," Ethel recounted bitterly, and Betty hated herself all over again for being the one to instigate this downward spiral. "I thought I actually *meant* something to him, you know? I thought he was this, like, amazing *artist*, and that we had a *connection*. Being with him made me feel special, but it turns out I was just his *side piece* the whole time!"

"Stop saying things like that." Betty switched the playlist, trying not to be obvious about it. "In fact, you need to stop letting yourself even *think* things like that. We have literally just finished establishing that you're a catch, and Bingo is a lying sleaze! He never deserved you, and you know it."

"Well, I know it *now*." Ethel sniffed, switching the playlist back. "Before, I thought he was this cool, dreamy musician, which is basically, like, my ideal guy, because—have I ever told you about this?"

"No." Betty reached for the settings to change the playlist again, and Ethel deftly grabbed her hand out of the air and held it. Her grip was warm and surprisingly strong.

"I had this dream—like an actual, for-real dream—when I was in sixth grade, about the guy I was going to marry." A wistful look overcame her, her gaze not focusing. "He had these big puppy-dog eyes and perfect hair, and he played guitar in a band, and I was just like . . . I always hoped that maybe it would be real someday, like maybe it was some kind of psychic thing, you know?"

"Wow," Betty remarked politely. Up above, the clouds were thinning, the moon peeking around their lacy edges. "That's intense."

"It was just a stupid dream," Ethel snorted, wincing slightly as she reached down to hold her stomach. "But I'd spent so long wishing for this perfect guy to be real, that when Bingo came along with his stupid hair and his stupid guitar, I really wanted to believe that it was him. I wanted it so bad I didn't even try to think about all the reasons why he was literally too good to be true."

"Stop saying he's 'too good,'" Betty commanded. "He's a dirtbag. He lied to you, and he lied to that Amber girl—who I sincerely hope is kicking his butt right now—and he has definitely not earned the right to this much space in your thoughts."

Ethel nodded distractedly, but she grabbed her stomach with both hands now, and Betty took advantage of the moment to switch the playlist again.

"Are you feeling okay?"

"Yeah. I think it's just cramps—because of *course* it is." The girl rolled her eyes, massaging her abdomen and taking slow, deliberate breaths. "I'm not even supposed to get my period for another week, but what the hell, right? Why not this on top of everything else? At least it's not ruining a *good* night."

Betty was silent for a moment, the clouds moving faster, the lace shredding to show the first twinkling stars she'd seen all night. Carefully, she asked, "So how long were you and Bingo dating?"

"Apparently we were never dating at all." Ethel gave a self-deprecating snort and then winced again, hunching over slightly. "*Ow*. But I guess if you want to be technical, we started talking, like, six weeks ago? We didn't actually hook up until Reggie's party last month, though—the one by the Wesley Road bridge." She sighed, her breathing a little shaky. "I thought he was, like, the perfect guy, and he just thought I was some kind of pathetic groupie, or something! I can't believe I trusted him."

"Ethel . . ." Betty began, but she didn't know how to finish what she had to say. Alarm bells were ringing in her ears so loudly she could barely hear herself think.

"You wanna know the punch line? He wasn't even a good kisser." Ethel forced a laugh that ended in a hiss as she doubled over in her seat, clutching her abdomen. Overhead, the clouds flew faster, kite tails streaming through brilliant moonlight. "All that swagger, all that cocky 'I'm with the band' crap, and it was like putting my face in a blender. He kisses with his freaking teeth."

They were just gliding past the municipal junkyard, a mountain range of refuse behind a tall, wooden fence, and Betty's foot slipped off the accelerator. "He . . . are you saying that Bingo . . . did he *bite* you?"

"I had to wear a turtleneck for a week," Ethel complained through locked jaws, and then she hunched over further, a rattling groan escaping from the depths of her throat. The clouds had scattered at last, chased away by the wind, revealing the full moon outside.

"Ethel?" Sweat tickled Betty's underarms when the girl didn't answer right away. "Talk to me, okay? What's happening, what's wrong?"

There was a crackling sound, multiple joints popping at once—and then Ethel's head snapped back in a sudden jerk, her neck bent at a freakish angle. Her nose twisted up and jutted forward, her back arched painfully, and a dull yellow light sparkled to life in her rolling eyes. Grinning at Betty with a mouth full of jagged, rapidly growing teeth, she snarled, *"I'm . . . HUNGRYYY."*

EIGHTEEN

SWEATY HANDS SLIPPING ON the wheel, Archie blinked into the darkness, fighting the urge to panic. He couldn't afford to lose Jughead now—if he had any hope of proving that his best friend wasn't the monster stalking Riverdale, he needed to catch up to him again.

And if Jughead *was* the monster stalking Riverdale . . . well, he still needed to catch up to him again.

Recklessly, he pressed down on the gas pedal, urging the sedan forward, examining the shadowy roadside for signs of a break in the trees that might indicate a cross street. Jughead couldn't have just *dematerialized*, or something, and his freaking bicycle definitely wasn't fast enough to outrun a car. Unless there was a hidden turnoff, he had to be somewhere ahead.

His fingers hovering over the switch for the headlights,

Archie began to perspire freely, afraid to turn them on and risk giving himself away, and just as afraid to keep them off and risk letting Jughead escape all together. Thanks to a month of training with Elena, he knew how to tuck and roll, how to aim for a moving target, and how to reload a gun while running for his life, but he had no idea how to make this call. Taking a deep breath, he grabbed hold of the switch and licked his lips, hoping he wasn't on the verge of making a huge mistake.

Just when he was about to go for it, something at the side of the road caught his eye, and Archie slammed his foot on the brake. Tires chirped against pavement, his little pine tree air freshener swinging wildly from the rearview mirror, and his seat belt locked tight across his chest as he skidded to a quick stop. Slamming the vehicle into reverse, he backed up until he was side by side with what he'd almost blown right past: a bicycle, tucked among the trees, only just visible in the growing light of the moon.

For a moment he just sat there, the four-door chugging away, waiting for . . . he wasn't even sure what. Jughead was nowhere to be seen, the bike propped against the trunk of a birch, abandoned, the wooded slope beyond climbing and vanishing into layers of black on gray. When Archie lowered the passenger window, a stiff wind whistled past, hurling a cluster of brittle, autumn leaves into the car; but it wasn't loud enough to disguise the sound of feet crashing through dried underbrush farther up the hillside.

Reversing a bit more, Archie parked his car on the shoulder of the road, killing the engine. Hands tight on the wheel, rocking back and forth in his seat, he pursed his lips into a knot and tried to give himself a silent pep talk. He needed to do this. He'd *promised* to do this. If Jughead was killing people, if he was truly responsible for the horrific fates that had befallen Dilton, Miss Grundy, and Pop Tate—not to mention an entire group of strangers at a campsite not a mile away from here—then he needed to be stopped. The Riverdale Ripper could not be permitted to kill anyone else.

Climbing out of the car, his fingers trembling, Archie double-checked the safety on his handgun. Then, he set off into the woods, following the sound of Jughead's footsteps.

👑👑👑

The sky was cloudless now, moonlight raining down from a field of black velvet, as the Beetle swerved wildly off the road. Gravel scattering beneath its directionless wheels, its chassis bouncing against fragmented pavement, the vehicle left the roadway and hurtled over the berm. Its headlights dipped down, shot up again, and then the front end plowed head-on into the trunk of a massive oak tree.

Metal screamed and crumpled, glass shattered, and the front axle snapped in half—while, inside the car, a werewolf tore through its half-shredded seat belt and slammed into the windshield so hard its neck snapped in three places. Even though she'd braced for the impact, the sudden eruption of the driver's side air bag caught Betty Cooper by surprise, hitting her with the force of a right hook.

Dazed and disoriented, her ears ringing and her vision full of bright, pulsing spots, Betty struggled through the confusion as the bag deflated. Beside her, Ethel was more wolf than girl, her limbs twitching, the remnants of her clothes hanging in shreds from her still-shifting body. Deadly claws tipped mutating hands that scrabbled against the dashboard, hair sprouted along the girl's neck and ears— and the bright yellow light in her eyes, which had dimmed when the crash broke her neck, was already starting to regain its strength.

Even while in the midst of yanking the wheel to the side, steering for the tree, and stomping down on the gas, Betty had known that the impact would be more likely to kill her than Ethel. *The only guaranteed ways to stop a werewolf are a silver bullet or a blade to the neck.* It had been little more than a desperate ploy to buy time—which was already running out. Before Betty's very eyes, her passenger's superhuman ability to heal was fixing the extensive damage caused by the crash.

With a hideous pop and crunch, Ethel's vertebrae realigned, and her expanding shoulders tore the remnants of her jacket into scraps.

Fumbling with her seat belt, it took Betty three tries to make the release work, the metal tongue finally slipping free from the buckle just as Ethel shoved herself back from the shattered windshield and worked the rest of her joints into place. Her face was completely misshapen now, her jaws stretched forward as her nose morphed into a snout, and her tongue slashed the air between them. Her blazing yellow eyes turned on Betty—and she lunged.

In a single, fluid motion, Betty hurled herself out of the car, landing on her back in the dirt and kicking the driver's side door closed again as hard as she could, bracing it with her legs. She was almost too late—Ethel moved so fast she already had one massive paw in the way when it slammed shut on her, and she was forced to retreat with a pained yelp. A half second later, though, the beast girl rammed against the door from the inside, with so much force that Betty felt the impact all the way up to her hips.

Sweat broke out at the blond girl's temples as she clutched at the earth, shoving her feet against the door with every ounce of strength she had. Ethel backed up and charged again, the vehicle rocking, the already cracked glass of the driver's side window exploding from its frame in a shower of fragments. Betty gasped, covering her eyes, her thighs trembling as pain rocketed up her legs. She wasn't going to be able to hold out much longer.

In a way, though, she was lucky. Ethel was so disoriented by the rapid changes overtaking her body—her altered center of gravity, her heightened senses, her reshaped limbs and stiff fingers—that her movements lacked the strength and coordination of a more experienced lycanthrope. In a matter of minutes, she'd regain enough of her agility to climb right through the shattered window. And with just another shift or two under her belt, the wolf-girl inside the car would have been thinking clearly enough to turn around and try the unblocked passenger-side door instead.

Ethel drew back and then launched forward one last time, and Betty took her feet off the door the instant before it crashed open wide, revealing the girl's fully changed form. Eyes burning, drool spilling between teeth like stalactites, Ethel gripped the doorframe with massive paws and prepared to pounce—but Betty was already yanking her revolver free from her purse, its remaining contents scattering everywhere, her finger closing on the trigger.

One, two, the shots were deafening, the scent of cordite and hot metal filling the air, the first silver bullet tearing through the roof of the Beetle and the second catching Ethel Muggs high in the left shoulder. Letting out an animalistic shriek, the wolf-girl hurtled back across the front seats, the vehicle rocking again as she smashed against the passenger window.

Her heart racing, her mouth dry, Betty kicked the driver's side door shut again and rolled to her feet, sprinting into the darkness—running for her life.

NINETEEN

IT WASN'T UNTIL HE HAD lost sight of the road behind him, shadows gathering like an army among the trees, that it finally occurred to Archie that he might be making a crucial mistake. The air was cold, the moon only visible in tiny shards through the dense network of naked branches overhead, and the distant rustle of Jughead's footsteps—the sound he'd been following—had stopped. He was alone now, in the middle of the woods on the track of a werewolf, having not thought to tell a single person where he was going. Oops?

Briefly, he considered sending Betty a text—*lost in the woods lol*—but decided not to bother. No matter what kind of trouble he was in, it was too late for anyone to come to his rescue, and it was high time he learned how to face it. Swallowing around a dry lump in his throat, he tested the weight of his handgun for the umpteenth time, trying to find its power of life and death reassuring. It wasn't. The time had long since passed that he could pretend his best friend wasn't the monster they were hunting—or that there could be any kind of reasonable, innocent explanation for this nighttime excursion to the woods.

And somewhere up ahead, Jughead might already be shedding his human skin, turning into the beast that left such gruesome crime scenes behind that three of the sheriff's deputies had quit their jobs in the last month. Taking several deep breaths to center himself, to steady his shaking hands, Archie pushed forward through the dried and tangled underbrush with the gun held out in front of him.

At the top of a short rise, the ground leveled off, the wooded slope giving way to a cleared trail that curved sinuously through the trees. In both directions, the path was eaten by darkness, and silence hung like a glass dome over the night. No footsteps disturbed the fallen leaves, no crickets chirruped from their hidden safety . . . if there was anything alive out there, other than Archie—and Jughead, wherever he was—it was *scared*.

The moon was still too obscured by the trees for him to see the ground, so Archie risked pulling out his cell phone, using the flashlight function to examine the earth at his feet. He saw where leaves had been swept out of the woods and onto the trail by careless feet, and the direction in which they'd been tracked, so he started walking. Trying to be stealthy, he shivered all over from more than just the deepening chill. Was Jughead coming out here to hunt the same grounds where he'd slaughtered those campers? Or was he planning to meet up with someone?

Was he possibly planning to meet up with a whole *pack* of someones?

Elena's library contained hundreds of facts and figures about lycanthropy—how the condition manifested itself, what its specific indications were, how werewolves behaved and how they could be killed. The literature noted repeatedly that wolves were pack animals and that even the supernatural kind preferred to hunt in groups whenever possible. No matter how many times Betty insisted it was uncommon for multiple werewolves to be romping around at the same time, for all Archie knew, he might be headed straight into the jaws of something truly heinous. Guilt racking his insides, he couldn't help the furtive hope that Bingo Wilkin might also be a monster after all, so that maybe Betty had been led out to this same patch of spooky, distant forest. Maybe he wouldn't have to face this alone.

The trail snaked through the trees and sloped upward, finally spilling into a small patch of cleared earth where birches, maples, and cedars were towering around the remains of a ruined building. What little was left of its stone walls framed a poured concrete floor, in the center of which was a dark hole that bristled with a small network of ancient pipes. It was a pump house, drawing water from a well that had—at some point in the past—surely been a vital resource for the lumberjacks that worked these woods.

On the ground beside the abandoned well, his back to the trailhead, sat Jughead Jones. His head was bowed, his shoulders slumped, and multiple lengths of heavy-duty chain had been strung around his chest, waist, and ankles, fixed to the metal pipes with a steel padlock the size of a fist. A cold wind rushed past, making the branches chitter around the clearing, and Archie lowered his gun before he even realized he'd aimed it.

"Go away." Choked and thick with tears, Jughead's voice was barely audible. He still hadn't turned around—hadn't even looked to see who was there behind him. "Go home, Archie. Don't ask me any questions, just . . . just go, okay? Please."

Letting out a breath that ended in a whimper, he curled onto his side, his shoulders shaking silently as the sharp wind swirled and danced around him. Archie went cold, the air pressed from his lungs, and he took a step backward. The gun in his hand felt heavy enough to pull his shoulder out of its socket. He had been planning to use the firearm, he realized; before he'd even fully made sense of what was in front of him, he'd already removed the safety and racked the slide, preparing to take his best friend's life.

Shame swept over him, and he almost dropped the weapon in the grass, wishing he'd never asked Elena to train him for this—wishing he'd never decided to leave his house at all the night he followed Betty to the secret gym. Remaining ignorant of the true dangers out there would still be better than *this*, than knowing what it felt like to be ready to kill someone you care about. While he'd been getting psyched up to pull a trigger, Jughead had been isolating himself in the deep woods, wrapping himself in chains so he couldn't hurt anyone. Maybe the guy was a killer after all . . . but he wasn't a monster. Only one of them had left home that night with the intention of shedding blood.

Archie fled from the clearing, not even looking for the trail, blundering into the woods too early and emerging along the road a quarter mile from his car. When he finally climbed behind the wheel, his chest was heaving and his eyes were too full of tears to see, so he put the gun back in his glove compartment, buried his face in his hands, and cried.

👑👑👑

The thing about running for your life is that you actually need a place to run to . . . and Betty didn't have one. She was miles from anywhere in either direction, and she'd definitely missed Ethel's heart with that shot. Any minute now, the werewolf-girl—probably ravenous after her first shift—would rip the silver bullet from her own shoulder; when she'd recovered from its poisonous effect on her system, also any minute now, she'd be out for vengeance, as well.

Betty should have pressed her advantage while she had it; she should have jumped up and emptied her gun into the car, stopping Ethel for good, and she knew it. It would have been the best tactical maneuver, and undoubtedly what Elena would have done. But missing two shots in a row had rattled her, and knowing she'd have no chance to reload—because the rest of her silver bullets were now strewn all over the ground beside the Beetle, along with everything else she'd kept in her bag—had rattled her further. On instinct, she'd bought time again, seeking a better position, a second chance with more favorable odds.

Just back from the roadside, the weather-beaten fence of the municipal junkyard rose like an ancient city wall, capped with coils of razor wire that gleamed viciously under the full moon. It was the only place for miles around that she might have a chance of finding more weapons, or at least a place to hide, and she sprinted for the gate across its front entrance. She hesitated for only a second before using her gun to blast open the lock—three bullets left, now—and shoved her way onto the lot.

Great dunes of plastic and metal rose before her under the moonlight, the wind carrying the scent of grease, earth, and decay, and she took a frantic look around. There were junked cars, oil drums filled with refuse, and a prefabricated structure just inside the entrance that housed a tiny office. Its door had a simple security mechanism, one she could easily pick if she only had the time to spare, but its walls could have been made from origami for how much protection they would offer against a hungry, furious werewolf.

As if on cue, the gate behind her smashed open a second time, and Betty whirled around to see the Ethel wolf charge onto the lot. Eyes bright, lips curled back to reveal every one of her sharp, glistening teeth, the monster-girl bounded forward and leaped suddenly sideways into the air. Betty swung the gun up and fired, the bullet slamming into the wooden fence as the beast landed and pivoted; dropping to one knee and spinning, Betty squeezed off a second shot that thumped into the side panel of an old Buick as Ethel bounded out of the way, back toward the office.

Too late, two more bullets wasted. Betty realized she was being baited into spending what remained of her ammunition; she had only one shot left, and Ethel was crouched low, panting and watching her—waiting to see if the girl would try again. For the first time, a true inkling of fear cut a cold path down Betty's back. She was great at hitting the targets in Elena's gym, when cardboard circles were sitting still and she was the one on the move, but this was completely different. Nothing could have prepared her for a moment like this one. Her mouth dry, her hands starting to shake, she knew that if she did try again, she would very likely miss.

Backing away, Betty inched toward one of the massive piles of rubbish that loomed in the middle of the yard, her eyes locked on Ethel. The werewolf-girl sidled out of the shadow of the office, creeping around one of the massive oil drums, and prowled a few steps closer. Betty braced herself, expecting another jump—which is why she was taken by surprise when her opponent spun instead, grabbing one of the heavy drums and throwing it with all her considerable strength.

The metal barrel sailed straight at Betty, fast-food wrappers and plastic bags flying loose from its open end, and the girl flung herself to the ground, diving narrowly out of the way as it slammed back down. She hadn't even stopped moving when Ethel came leaping after the makeshift missile, eyes gleaming as she dropped out of the sky, and Betty barely swerved back the other way in time. The werewolf's jaws missed her throat by only a hairbreadth as they snapped shut on thin air, saliva speckling the dusty earth.

Rolling up to her knees again, thrusting out the revolver

in a move she'd practiced a thousand times, Betty was still a beat too slow to take the kill shot—and a few inches too close to her target. Sweeping out with one elongated, muscular arm, Ethel caught her square in the chest with a blow that sent the girl flying, her body completely leaving the ground.

Limbs flailing, Betty came down hard on a nest of scrap metal and plastic sheeting, halfway up one of the mountainous heaps of refuse. The revolver slipped from her hand, vanishing among the debris, and a sharp impact against the back of her head made lights flash behind her eyes. The world spun as she struggled to drag herself upright again, the werewolf-girl already starting to climb up after her, tin cans and rusting hardware shifting precariously beneath her paws.

With a gasp, Betty shuffled backward, kicking loose a cascade of shrapnel as she retreated farther up the unstable hill. Ethel tried to jump, claws scrabbling for purchase; but the loose footing gave way beneath her, and she slid to the bottom again. Sweat rolling down her neck, Betty pulled herself up higher, grabbing on to the exposed springs of a rotting mattress, stumbling when a coil of wire wrapped around her ankle. Desperately, she looked for a weapon; it was a pile of metal, and there was only so high she could go—only so long until the wolf figured out a way up.

Ethel started again, trying a new section of the mound, scrambling up several feet before the scrap gave way and she backslid again. Wildly, Betty dug into the tangled debris at her feet, yanking loose an ancient hotplate, which she hurled at the werewolf's head. She followed it with a dented tire rim, a box grater, and a handful of roofing nails; and even though Ethel dropped further back with each direct hit, they clearly had no lingering effect, the growl in the beast's inhuman throat growing only deeper and more determined.

Inching higher, two-thirds of the way up, Betty searched desperately for a knife among the waste—or even a pole—anything she could use to fight back. Even if she couldn't kill Ethel, she could fend her off, or maybe wear her out . . . buy time until the inevitable. She had just uncovered a set of golf clubs when the wolf-girl finally threw something back, an old CPU smashing into the debris just beneath where Betty was standing, a depth charge that knocked her footing loose.

The girl toppled and rolled, her clothes ripping open on coat hangers and jutting L-brackets, and she narrowly avoided getting skewered by a windshield wiper before slamming down on a hard bed of sheet metal. The air was driven from her lungs, pain stabbing up and down the length of her sternum, and the night wobbled again as she gazed down to see the monster that was Ethel Muggs backing up across the junkyard lot—getting ready to take a running start.

In only three bounds the beast had built up the momentum she needed to launch herself into the air, soaring up and up and then down in a graceful arch; her claws stretched out and her teeth aimed for the vulnerable throat of her human prey. Running on adrenaline and instinct, Betty barely managed to drag a piece of sheet metal free, to swing it around with its slender, jagged edge aimed upward, in time to meet the werewolf as she landed.

Ethel's throat sank down onto the makeshift blade, blood spraying out of the wound and over Betty's face in a revolting bath of hot, slippery fluid. Surprise made the monster's eyes go wide, but it was too late; weight and momentum plunged her the rest of the way down, gristle and soft tissue splitting quickly apart until the metal sheet passed between two of the vertebrae in her neck . . . and the wolf-girl's head separated cleanly from her body.

It toppled forward, bouncing off Betty's shoulder and rolling down the slope of cast-off metal, while the rest of her went limp and heavy on top of the blond girl's torso. Tossing the sticky, impromptu weapon aside, her stomach heaving, Betty barely dragged herself free in time to puke her guts out into the basin of a discarded toilet.

👑👑👑

The buzzing of the phone in his pocket is what woke Archie up this time, his neck stiff, his fingers sluggish with cold as he rubbed his eyes. He was still parked at the side of the desolate, darkened road, the car so frigid he was surprised his breath didn't come out in visible puffs, and he was almost shocked to see how much time had passed when he finally wrestled his cell out into the open. Betty was calling.

"*I just killed Ethel Muggs!*" she screamed down the line, before he even had a chance to say hello.

"You . . . what?" Archie blinked a few times, trying to shake off the grogginess. "Betts, what—"

"Bingo is the wolf—it has to be him!" Betty sounded utterly distraught, nerves crackling in her voice like electrical interference. "I ran into Ethel at the bowling alley, and it turns out she and Bingo had a, a *Thing*, or something, only he bit her, and she . . . she *changed*. Archie, she transformed right in front of me, in my car!"

"Are you okay?" His brain wasn't moving fast enough to absorb what she was saying. *Ethel Muggs turned into a werewolf?* Archie could picture the girl, easily—someone he'd shared classrooms with for most of his life, always hovering just outside their inner circle—but he couldn't imagine what he was being told. "Did she hurt you?"

"I'm okay, but I'm not *okay*." Tears threatened Betty's voice, and he heard her swallow them back. "She tried to kill me, and I—she's dead, Archie."

She started explaining her evening, from running into Ethel at The Bingoes' gig to the reason she had the girl in her Beetle in the first place. As she reached the horrible moment when the girl's body began to reshape itself while they were trapped together on the way back to Riverdale, Archie shoved open his door and got out of the car. He'd never meant to fall asleep, and Betty's agitation was contagious; suddenly, all he could think about was how long it had been since he'd left Jughead alone in that clearing. With the gun gripped tightly in his hand, he hurried back into the trees and up the slope.

"I had to leave her body in the junkyard," Betty was finally saying as he reached the trailhead, the pump house ruins stark beneath the unguarded moon. "She was already beginning to shift back again, and it's . . . I mean, it's bad. Like, whatever you're imagining, make it ten times worse and you're still not there yet." She let out a shaky breath. "But my car is totaled, and now I'm stranded out here with a headless corpse."

Archie's lips were stiff, his voice strained and unnatural when it eked out between them. "Betts, I can't—"

"I don't know what to do," she blurted. "My parents are out of town, Elena is somewhere hunting Jacob, and I need to get back to Midville before the band finishes their set. I don't want you to have to leave Juggie, but I need a ride!"

"Okay, well, uh . . . I guess I've got good news and bad news," Archie replied nervously. Turning a quick 360, he scanned the entire area, the gun bobbing a little in his unsteady hand. What remained of the pump house walls were right where he remembered them—but the rusting metal pipes had been ripped clean out of the ground, and the heavy chains that had once been wrapped tightly around his best friend's waist were now strewn across the clearing. Empty. "Because Jughead is gone."

TWENTY

TWO MILES AWAY, BREATHING hard through the muscle cramps that racked his entire body, Jughead Jones stumbled over a fallen log and crashed to the forest floor. The pain was literally blinding, a shimmering curtain of wobbly light distorting the world as agony lanced him from every angle. He forced air into his lungs down a knotted windpipe, battling against his body, his instincts, with everything he had.

His hands convulsed, the knuckles swelling and sprouting hair—only to shrink again a moment later, as he put every bit of concentration he could into fighting the transformation. His shoulders were wider than they should be, his torso stretched and his face misshapen, but the worst were his legs. His knees kept snapping back and forth, the bones and ligaments rearranging themselves over and over, the pain so excruciating he was afraid he'd black out.

He wanted to black out.

He couldn't afford to black out.

Back in the clearing, he'd lost control, breaking the lead pipes like carrot sticks and flinging aside the chains meant for his own protection—for everyone's protection. He'd covered a full mile before managing to claw his way through the mind-numbing haze, forcing back the beast, regaining some part of himself. But he was losing the war, and he knew it. The moon pulled at him, gravity drawing the wolf to the surface, and he couldn't stand the torture of resisting it much longer.

A deep rumble shook his stomach, hunger making him dizzy, and his knuckles swelled again. He couldn't stop them this time.

Something bad was going to happen.

When Betty Cooper jumped into his car from where she'd been waiting beside her demolished Beetle, Archie just narrowly stifled the urge to scream out loud. She looked horrendous—her clothes ripped and filthy, her face bruised and streaked with hastily mopped blood— but she didn't even wait until her seat belt was buckled before ordering him to start driving.

"We're gonna be late," she reported ominously, an edge of fear to her voice Archie hadn't heard before. In her hand, Betty clutched a pile of dusty silver bullets, and as soon as they were moving she started reloading her gun. "The Bingoes are probably done with their gig already, and then . . ."

She didn't finish, and into the guilty silence, Archie blurted, "I'm sorry, Betts. I shouldn't have left Jug alone, I should have—"

"Don't." She met his eyes, her expression pained but gentle. "Seriously, Archie, don't blame yourself. It's your first time doing this, and you made a bad call—it happens. I did the same thing when all those people died in the woods and I decided it wasn't my mess to clean up." Slumping back in her seat, she closed her eyes. "I should have stepped up, but I was scared I wasn't ready. So I let Elena add it to the list of everything else she's dealing with right now, and . . . well, here we are."

"This isn't your fault, either, you know," he returned with a careful frown. "I mean, I'm not even ready to take that chemistry exam next week—it's probably okay if you weren't prepared to become Riverdale's monster hunter in chief over summer break."

She wasn't ready to give up her self-recrimination, though. "Monsters don't care whether you're prepared or not."

"You can't anticipate literally everything all the time, Betts. And it's not like you sat back and let werewolves take over, either—you *did* take charge, and you even recruited your first deputy!"

He made a grand gesture at himself, and Betty rolled her eyes with a good-humored grin. But then she became somber again. "What if I'm still not ready?"

"If you weren't ready, you wouldn't have made it out of that junkyard alive," Archie pointed out softly. "Whatever you think you have to prove, you *proved* it." When she didn't answer right away, he added, "And for what it's worth? I would trust you with my life. I mean, uh . . . I guess I kind of *am* trusting you with my life." Reaching over, he gave her shoulder a friendly nudge. "Seriously, though, Betts. You're kinda my hero."

She didn't say anything—just flipped down the passenger-side visor and started trying to clean the rest of Ethel's blood off her face—but out of the corner of his eye, Archie could see a small, private smile tugging at her lips.

They didn't say much for the rest of the drive back to the bowling alley, tension filling the car like slowly rising water, replacing all the oxygen in the air. There were two werewolves out there, somewhere, and they'd lost track of them both. Whatever his intentions were when he'd chained himself up in the woods, Jughead had escaped his own safety precautions—and with Bingo's gig by now almost certainly over, who knew where he might be? Neither Archie nor Betty wanted to bring up worst-case scenarios yet, but neither of them had the energy for optimism, and so they remained silent.

The lot outside Coney's Bowl-o-Rama was still fairly crowded when they pulled in, and Betty all but sprinted for the door as soon as Archie put the car into park. Inside, the air buzzed with loud conversation punctuated by the clatter of pins, but the only music that played was prerecorded, pumped through speakers mounted at ceiling level. Leading them to a bar at one end of the building, Betty cursed out loud when she took in the small performance-space setup in the corner—empty and dark.

Shoving her way around the room, she checked every face there, growing increasingly distressed when it became clear that Bingo was not among the remaining crowd. There were two boys their age seated at the counter, however, sharing what was left of a giant platter of nachos, and a measure of relief finally crossed her expression when she noticed them. Claiming the stool next to the guy on the left, whose T-shirt featured a stuffed cartoon bear holding a switchblade, Betty turned on a million-watt grin.

"Hey! You're Tough Teddy, right? From the band?"

The boy glanced over, gave her an appraising look, and

then offered a smile that he had probably practiced in the bathroom mirror a few hundred times. "That's me. Why? You want something autographed?"

"Maybe later." Betty gestured around the bar. "Listen, do you know where Bingo is?"

"Oh." His smile dropped faster than a guillotine. "You're one of Bingo's fans."

"Sort of. Not exactly." Betty's own grin faded as frustration crept into her tone. "Listen, I was here for your first set, but then I had to take a friend home, and I only just got back. She knows Bingo really well, and she wanted me to give him a message, but I don't know where he is."

Teddy ate another nacho, taking his sweet time chewing and swallowing before he decided to answer her. "Well, we don't know where he is, either. Some girl threw a drink on him during our break, and then he and his girlfriend had some words, and *she* threw a drink on him, and then he had a diva fit and said he had to go. So we never played the second set."

"You didn't?" Betty blinked, her back going straight.

"Nope." Teddy ate another nacho. "They pay us in food and free games, though, so Buddy and I have been hanging out and making the most of it. You're welcome to join us, if you want." Then he jerked a thumb in Archie's direction. "Unless this dude is your boyfriend. Single chicks only."

"Thanks for the tempting offer," Betty said mildly, "but the food here looks kind of disgusting, and this message is really urgent. Any idea where Bingo went when he left?"

"Your guess is as good as mine." Teddy gave a half-hearted shrug that made it clear he wasn't going to be making any guesses and then turned back to his bandmate to continue the conversation they'd been having when Betty interrupted.

"Damn." Facing Archie again, the girl slammed her fist down on the counter. "*Damn!*"

"Don't panic, Betts, it's not too late," Archie said, swallowing the words *I hope*. "We can still find them."

"Yeah. Okay." She cast one more glance around the bar and then nodded, a grim set to her jaw. "Let's go."

Together, they raced back through the bowling alley and out into the parking lot, the full moon watching them like a judgmental eye.

👑👑👑

Music played softly from the wireless speaker on the bathroom counter as Bingo Wilkin shut off the taps in the shower, a tingle building in his fingers. In fact, the tingle was building everywhere, his blood itching with the need to shift, his body desperate to claim its true form. Just thinking about it made coarse hair sprout on his chest, the bones of his shoulders and rib cage aching with the urge to transform themselves. Drawing slow, deep breaths, he fought it back.

It wasn't time yet.

Stepping out of the tub, he grabbed a towel and dried off. Maybe it had been silly to take a shower, since his plans for the evening included morphing into a creature of nightmares and bathing himself in the blood of his next meal, but the soda had made his hair sticky, and he couldn't stand the way it felt. His mouth twisted into a perversely delighted smile at the memory. *Betty Cooper.* He'd never realized what a spitfire she was. Maybe it was her who he ought to have been pursuing all this time.

Dressing in loose-fitting clothes—things he could take off again without too much trouble, once his limbs started being a little less cooperative—he made his way to the kitchen, where a digital clock showing the late hour glowed in the darkness. He was just reaching for the light switch when he paused, his eyes narrowing as they drank in the shadows that filled the room. Aside from the hum of the refrigerator, everything was silent; his parents were out, and he was home alone.

Or at least he was supposed to be.

"Jughead?" Bingo smiled into the dark, the itch in his

blood just a little bit stronger. "I know you're here—I can smell you. Come out, come out, wherever you are . . ."

Two yellow lights blazed to life in the far corner of the room, a tall, misshapen figure staggering into view from behind a freestanding cabinet, moving to just where the light from the hall could touch him. Muscles writhed and rippled across Jughead's bare chest and arms, his body caught painfully between its two forms, and he glared at Bingo with undisguised loathing. His shoulders were covered in hair, his hands knobby and clawed, and his face was twisted into a nearly unrecognizable shape.

And yet he still wore that ridiculous hat.

"Hello, cousin." Bingo flipped on the kitchen lights, smirking as Jughead flinched from the sudden brightness, his eyes hypersensitized by their own unearthly glow. "I was wondering how long it would take you to seek out your pack."

"What . . ." Jughead struggled to speak, his voice gruff and guttural, his words strangled by the inhuman structure of his altered throat. "What . . . did you . . . *do to me?*"

"Me? Nothing." Bingo crossed to the sink, smiling, acting nonchalant—but he kept the small kitchen table between the two of them, just in case. It wouldn't slow a determined werewolf down for more than a second . . . but these days, Bingo didn't need much more time than that to complete his own change. "Your *genes* did this, buddy. *Our* genes. It's a lot to take in, I know, especially in the beginning, but it's part of your DNA, just like your pasty skin and dark hair."

Jughead shuffled a little closer, breathing hard, one of his legs bent back the wrong way. "You . . . made me . . . kill people!"

"I didn't make you do anything." Bingo got a glass down from the cabinet, his hands burning now, Jughead's proximity making his own werewolf blood howl in his veins. "Two months ago, you found me on the night of your first change, hungry and wild; I took you into the woods, I taught you how to hunt without getting caught or killed, and you had the meal of your life. You're welcome for that, by the way."

A fist came down on the kitchen table with so much force the surface cracked, and Bingo turned to see his cousin quivering with rage. "You're the reason . . . those people . . . are dead! You . . . I . . . I didn't want . . . to, t-to . . ."

"You didn't want to?" Bingo laughed heartily before gulping some of the water. "Keep telling yourself that if you need to hear it, but it's a load of crap." He set the glass down on the counter with a loud *clunk*. "Hunting is a natural instinct for our kind, and you were going to kill whether I helped you do it or not. And don't give me that disgusted look, either, because I might be the only other person who knows exactly what happened to Pop Tate. You and I have the same dark side, buddy."

"That was . . . an accident." Jughead's shoulders sagged miserably, his voice reduced to nearly a whisper. "I n-never . . . never meant to . . . never wanted to—"

"Yes, you did." Bingo rolled his eyes, finally losing his patience. "Of course you *meant to* kill him—of course you *wanted to*. You're a *predator*, Jughead Jones! I didn't force you to wait inside that crypt so you could ambush your buddy Dilton. I didn't make you rip his liver out with your teeth. I didn't hypnotize you into chasing Grundy into our trap, and I definitely didn't set you loose in the Chock'Lit Shoppe. That was all you, man, and the sooner you embrace it, the happier you'll be."

"Happy?" Jughead's eyes blazed, and he grabbed one of the kitchen chairs, hurling it across the room and into the shelves above the stovetop. Coffee cups shattered, cookbooks spilling to the floor, and the violence sent adrenaline racing through Bingo's system. His cousin snarled balefully. "You think . . . I could ever be . . . happy *again*? Like *this*?"

"Well. Not with that attitude." Bingo crossed his arms over his chest.

Jughead let out a growl that turned into a roar, and he picked up another chair, flinging it into the refrigerator. The stainless-steel door of the appliance dented, the makeshift missile fracturing, and magnets rained to the floor. Wheeling around, the muscles in his face convulsing as his nose and ears stretched another centimeter into their new shape, Jughead exclaimed wildly, "We . . . we killed people!"

"And we'll kill more." Bingo grinned. "And eventually you'll get good at it."

"I don't . . . want to!" Jughead was gasping for air, his rage pulling energy away from his fight against the shift. "Make it . . . *stop!* We have to . . . keep it . . . from happening—"

"Haven't you been listening to me at all?" Bingo slipped his shirt over his head. The moment was coming when his own resistance would crumble, and he was ready for it, the tendons in his neck jutting out already as his body started giving in to its own transformation. "There is no stopping it! And even if a way existed, even if I *could* do it, I wouldn't." His bones cracked as they expanded, his skin pulling and stretching, but it felt like relief.

"You're so pathetic, you know that? You're turning into something better, faster, and stronger than a mere human *right now*, but you're still fighting it every step of the way. Stop feeling sorry for *people*, Jughead—they're nothing! I'm glad I am what I am."

A million pinpricks danced up his arms as fur began to poke through the skin, and he stepped out of his pants just as the muscles in his legs began to knot and swell. Jughead was still clinging to the last vestiges of his human appearance, but his battle was nearly lost. Still, he managed to rasp, "You're . . . a monster."

"I'm just like you," Bingo returned with a gleeful laugh, his spine crackling as it lengthened, his ears rising into points. "And I know how hungry you're feeling right about now. So what do you say, cousin? Up for a bite tonight?"

Jughead's chest heaved, a tail sweeping the air as what remained of his jeans split apart, and he snarled, "Maybe I am."

With that, he tossed the kitchen table aside with a mighty crash and lunged forward, jaws stretching and snapping—his jutting teeth primed for Bingo's jugular.

TWENTY-ONE

"I NEVER SHOULD HAVE TAKEN my eyes off him!" Betty exclaimed, throwing herself into the passenger seat of Archie's car and squeezing her head between her hands. Outside, the night was still and perfect, a single feathered cloud traveling under the bright disc of the moon—but all she could see was red. "If I'd just stayed at the stupid bar, if I hadn't been so dead set on proving what a scumbag Bingo was being—"

"Then Ethel would have ended up changing into a were-wolf in the middle of a bowling alley filled with people," Archie finished for her as he buckled his seat belt. "Even if that wasn't why you did it, you still probably saved a whole bunch of lives."

Betty thought for a moment, her eyes narrowed. "That isn't the point and you know it, but you're deliberately making it hard for me to argue with you."

"Guilty." He smiled, putting the car into gear and reversing out of their parking spot. "You're gonna drive yourself nuts if you second-guess all your choices like this. You lost sight of Bingo, but you prevented a bloodbath—and now that we know who the werewolves are, we still have a chance to stop them."

Unspoken words filled the car as they reached the mouth of the lot, Archie's headlights spearing out into the night. Softly, Betty said, "I'm sorry. I know I've said it before, but I really am sorry we have to go after Juggie."

"Yeah, well." Archie looked away, shifting uncomfortably. "It was always going to end up being somebody's best friend, right? Might as well be mine." An empty smile tugged up one corner of his mouth when he finally turned back to face her. "Anyway, you know what they say: 'Sometimes you have to kill to be kind.'"

It was a saying he'd learned from Elena, of course, and Betty nodded the way she had every time she'd heard it out of her aunt's mouth. She wanted to ask if Archie really would be ready to kill when the time came . . . but she was afraid he'd say no. The truth she really didn't want to admit out loud was that she might *also* say no if he asked her the same thing. The memory of Ethel's final moments was impossible to escape from—and even though she'd had no other choice at the time but to defend herself, she'd killed someone she knew. It wasn't an experience she was anxious to repeat. Ever. And especially not in the next few hours.

"So," Archie finally said, after they'd each been sitting uncomfortably with their thoughts for a while. "Where are we going, anyway?"

His car was still idling at the exit of the bowling alley parking lot, the crisp night inappropriately peaceful around them, and Betty drummed her fingers on the dashboard. "Where was the last place you saw Juggie?"

"It was in the woods, not far from the campgrounds." Archie stared up at the moon. "I guess he might still be out there. As far as I know, that whole area is still closed to visitors, so there shouldn't be any people around tonight. If we're lucky, maybe he's just hunting deer and rabbits?"

"We're not lucky." If Betty was certain of anything, it was that. "They could have gone after deer and rabbits last month, but they didn't. They know exactly what kind of prey they want, and they'll go where they can find it."

Archie winced a little, understanding what she meant. "So, Riverdale, then?"

"I'm not sure." Betty turned back around, looking at the lit-up frontage of Coney's Bowl-o-Rama. "Wolves are pack animals, and it takes lycanthropes a while to develop the kind of self-control they need to override their animal instincts. If Juggie changed and escaped while you were in your car, there's a pretty decent chance that the first thing he did was go looking for Bingo."

"Oh, man." Archie ran his fingers through his hair, making it stand on end. "Last month, the only reason I went to Reggie's stupid party was because of Jug. He told me he thought Bingo might be there, and he needed to see him."

"They were together when I found them," Betty confirmed, thinking back to that night by the Wesley Road bridge—to the way Bingo insisted Jughead take her home. *"Maybe you and Betty should stop for a bite on the way."* An involuntary shiver shot through her all the way down to her toes as she was thrown by a sudden, disturbing realization. She blinked twice, her heart sinking beneath an enormous weight, wishing that she was wrong—and knowing that she wasn't. "Bingo was the one in control. He left first, on his own, and kind of made a point out of it. He wanted Juggie to be by himself that night, so there wouldn't be another were-wolf around to help him stay in control once he shifted and the hunger set in." Her voice thin and faraway, she struggled to articulate the next thought. "He meant for Juggie to eat *me*."

Archie turned pale. "You really think so?"

"One of the reasons werewolves eventually embrace the beast within is because they can't handle the guilt anymore," Betty said softly, looking down at her hands. There was still blood under her nails. "All that death, and no one to blame but themselves? The fastest way to escape the horror is to lean into it. You saw what a mess he was after Pop Tate died—now imagine if the person he'd killed was one of his oldest friends."

Archie swallowed a few times before he seemed to find his voice again. "Okay. Okay, so . . . Jug probably went after Bingo. But where did *he* go?"

"Like you said, the woods are probably empty. Most of Riverdale really rolls up the sidewalks after dark these days, and Sheriff Keller has extra patrol cars on the streets—so if Bingo's smart, he's probably staying local."

"Makes sense," Archie allowed. "I'm not super familiar with Midville, though. And I definitely haven't spent enough time with Bingo to guess who he'd target if he decided to go after people he knows."

"Have you ever been to his house?" Betty asked. "If his parents are at home, maybe we can bluff them and get some ideas."

"I've been there once." Archie scrunched up his nose, thinking. "It was a while ago, but I bet I could find the neighborhood again."

"Okay, then." Betty took a breath, felt her heartbeat picking up. "We have a plan. Right? We go to Bingo's, and . . . on the way, we figure out what we'll say when we get there."

"Perfect," Archie agreed, sounding wholly unconvinced. He pulled out of the parking lot at last, heading in the direction of Midville.

Jughead had rage on his side, but not experience. He was in midair when he finished his transformation, but by the time his jaws closed around his cousin's neck, Bingo's throat was already protected by a thick pelt of charcoal-and-silver fur. They crashed to the ground, rolling across the tile, and Jughead's teeth slipped free from their hold. Slamming into the cabinets beneath the sink, he scrambled to right himself again while his cousin danced out of reach.

Bingo had backed away, stepping in a careful semicircle, snarling down at him—waiting. The voice inside that belonged to Jughead's human self, the one of reason and rationale, was gone. In its place was only a feral need for blood, for *dominance*, and he could silence it no longer. There would be no walking away from this fight, no matter how outclassed he was. He would either defeat his cousin, or he would die trying.

And he hadn't even begun to try.

Shoving against the baseboard with his hind feet, he leaped into the air again, jaws sharp and wide. Bingo tried to feint, but it was a maneuver Jughead anticipated, and he managed to sink his teeth into one of his cousin's flanks. Blood welled up from the wound, warm and slippery, and the taste made his head spin with adrenaline and primal excitement. But his bite was still too shallow. With a piercing yelp, Bingo rolled, bracing his massive hind paws under Jughead's chest and sending him hurtling across the room.

Twice his normal size, and packed with dense, lean muscle, Jughead crashed into the Wilkins' vintage oven like a wrecking ball. The antique appliance caved in under the impact, breaking free from its moorings and scraping across the floor, ripping up the tile. A pipe that jutted from the wall gave off a soft hiss, pouring invisible gas into the air as Jughead shook himself out again, once more struggling up onto his feet.

The kitchen was already covered in wreckage—broken glass and ceramics, splintered fragments of wood from the table and chairs, books and magnets and bits of damaged flooring—but Bingo sat in the middle of it all, crouched calmly on his haunches, watching his cousin with amusement dancing in his eyes. His attitude was knowing, taunting, his relaxed pose a middle finger. *I could do this all day.*

Memories were coming back to Jughead, but still so much was a blur. That night in the woods two months ago . . . had that been the first time he ever changed? Had he claimed other victims no one even knew about? His subhuman consciousness teemed with an understanding of the silent communication that passed between wolves; he recalled the signals he'd obeyed, the instincts he'd honed, in just a few short nights under Bingo's tutelage. But he had no fighting experience, and his cousin knew it.

Growling deep in his throat, Jughead bared his teeth, rage at this unfairness quickly overpowering his common sense. With a start, Bingo rose onto all fours, backing away—and stumbling. His hind leg, on the side where he'd been bitten, gave out, and he fell into a seated position again. More adrenaline flooded Jughead's system, the show of weakness triggering an immediate impulse to seize the advantage, to strike . . . but that fading human voice inside urged him just as clearly to stop.

The competing instincts confused him, fogged his thoughts, leaving him briefly immobilized; and after a few endless moments, Bingo got up again, a sly look angling his features—his hind leg just fine. It had been a ruse, a trick meant to fool his cousin into making a hasty attack that he would regret. Folding his ears back, Jughead growled again, a low, threatening rumble that rattled the glasses on the counter. *No more games.* They circled each other, stepping over the sharp-edged debris that littered the floor, the number display shifting on the digital clock. And then Bingo lunged.

Their teeth clashed in a razor-tipped fury, their claws tearing vicious grooves in each other's flesh, and Jughead's pulse quickened when his fangs carved a notch out of Bingo's left ear. His cousin retreated with a sharp cry . . . and then charged again, immediately, and they raged throughout the kitchen. Slamming into drawers and counters, struggling for supremacy, they brought dishes down from the overhead cupboards while the air turned heavy and sweet with gas from the exposed line.

Bingo's smug confidence disappeared gradually, his scent turning sour, and the more blows he failed to land, the more erratic his movements became. When he made another leaping attack, it was finally Jughead's turn to feint. Darting left and then twisting right, he caused his cousin to overshoot the mark, and when their bodies collided, he buried his deadly teeth deep into Bingo's left shoulder. Their bodies rolled again, sliding through broken dishes, careening into the doorway that led to the living room.

Once again, Jughead tasted blood . . . and this time he wasn't going to be shaken off so easily. He bit down harder as Bingo scrabbled against the slick floor beneath them, feeling the shift of ligaments between his teeth, the resistance of bone; his jaw ached, but he clamped down with even more strength—as much as he could muster—his mind filling with ugly memories: *Dilton's mouth gaping open in death; Miss Grundy running in fear; Pop Tate's terrified, reeling eyes.* A frantic, high-pitched noise hung in the air, but Jughead ignored it, wrenching his head from side to side, tasting victory at last.

There was a hideous sound as the shoulder joint separated, as flesh sucked apart from flesh; and when Bingo finally braced his feet against his cousin's chest, kicking him away with everything he had, his arm ripped clean from his body. Jughead flew backward, the detached limb still clenched in his jaws, tumbling wildly into the living room and slamming into a wooden bench arranged beneath the picture window. Blood soaked the fur around his mouth, dripped from his whiskers, and he spat the appendage onto the floor.

Still in the kitchen, Bingo staggered backward, eyes bright, blood spurting from the massive wound in his shoulder. He crashed hard against the cabinet that stood in the corner, the digital clock teetering precariously before it toppled and finally fell. When it hit the ground, the plastic casing shattered, and a spark flashed around the base of the cord.

Their gazes met across the length of two rooms, their eyes widening as the gas-filled air crackled and a sound like a great, heaving gasp filled the house . . .

TWENTY-TWO

LEAFLESS TREES CLAWED THE AIR on either side of the road, streetlamps gilding their branches in tawny light as Archie and Betty drove slowly along the curb. The houses they passed were unremarkable to the point of being nearly indistinguishable: two stories, picture windows, gabled roofs . . . one after another, they repeated themselves like Russian dolls. The only thing that set any of them apart was whether a light was on inside.

"I'm pretty sure this is the right neighborhood," Archie declared, squinting at the row of identical mailboxes that lined the street, and Betty gritted her teeth so hard something popped in her jaw.

"I don't want to be the one to point this out, but there's nobody else, so I guess I'll have to: That's the third time you've said that," she remarked. Then: "Not that I'm criticizing! You're doing a great job, Archie. I'm sure we'll find it."

"Ugh," Archie groaned. "Don't be nice to me, it makes the guilt worse. If I were doing a great job, we'd be there already."

"What do you remember about Bingo's house?" Betty asked helpfully. She'd posed this question a half-dozen times already, but she was running out of clever ways to jog Archie's memory, and time was most definitely of the essence. "What color was it? What was the layout like, and was it on a corner, or . . .?"

"The house was . . . dark," Archie said confidently. "And it had two stories and a picture window. And a mailbox."

"Great." Betty felt her smile tighten a little bit. "That's . . . great. We're starting to narrow it down."

The car screeched to a sudden halt, and Betty's seat belt snapped tight against her shoulder. She was still catching her breath when Archie leaned across her, his eyes going wide. "And it had a birdhouse in the front yard, just like this one! I think this is it!"

Betty looked out at an unremarkable two-story home with a gabled roof, a featureless mailbox, and a birdhouse mounted on a post at the foot of the front walk. The place had a large picture window, like all the other houses on the block, but a light glowed somewhere inside . . . and a shadow moved across the glass.

"I think someone is home," she observed. And an instant later, a large figure smashed clean through the window, hurtling out from inside the house in a hail of deadly shards.

Hitting the ground in a frenzied roll, its giant paws flailing, a gargantuan brown wolf with glowing yellow eyes scrabbled to a desperate stop on the front lawn only a few feet from the sidewalk. It looked up, meeting Archie's and Betty's slack-jawed stares—scarcely a moment before a massive explosion shook the entire neighborhood.

The house blew apart from the baseboards, great billows of orange flame blasting out the windows and licking at the night, the impact so tremendous it made Archie's car rock on its axles. Wood and glass rained down from above, bits of smoldering insulation drifting on the air like hellish snow-flakes, and a plume of ugly black smoke mushroomed into the sky. Betty was still blinking in shock, blood roaring in her ears like a subway train, when the werewolf turned and sprinted up the street.

"W-what the . . .?" Archie's eyes were so wide they were in danger of falling out as he stared at the burning wreckage. "Did somebody just drop a *bomb* on Bingo's house?"

"Archie!" Betty gripped his shoulder, gesturing frantically out the windshield. "The wolf? He's getting away!"

The boy's eyes were still locked on the conflagration before them, his hands so tight on the steering wheel they looked like it would take surgery to pry them off. "Who do you think it was? Bingo, or . . . or Jug?"

"*Who the hell cares, just drive!*" Betty shouted, shoving his right leg down so his foot slammed onto the gas pedal. The car lurched forward with a sharp squeal from the tires, the front bumper narrowly missing the Wilkins' mailbox before Archie remembered that he was supposed to be steering. He corrected at the last second, and they took off down the street, flames licking at the treetops behind them.

👑👑👑

Chasing a werewolf is no easy task, even if you've had experience—and Archie had none. The beast moved with astonishing speed, its muscular limbs churning, its substantial feet allowing it to turn on a dime and change course without warning. Three blocks from Bingo's neighborhood, emergency sirens already wailing in the distance, Betty yanked her gun from her bag and then rolled down the window.

Unbuckling her seat belt, she said, "Try to keep as steady as possible, okay, Archie?"

"Betty, what do you—" But there was no point finishing; she was already half outside the car, her upper body leaning into the night, her blond ponytail streaming in the cold, unrelenting wind.

The werewolf was kicking up grit maybe twenty yards ahead, and Archie watched from the corner of one eye as Betty took aim, sighting down the barrel of her revolver. Then, just as she pulled the trigger, the beast veered right unexpectedly. The bullet slammed into the ground, ripping a hole out of the pavement, while their quarry vaulted the curb and streaked away from the road—unharmed.

"Damn!" The girl cursed, dropping back into her seat as Archie slowed the car, watching the wolf gallop across someone's yard, vanishing into the darkness that passed between houses. Gesturing wildly once again, Betty yelped, "What are you waiting for? Go! *Go go go!*"

"How?" Archie stared at the evenly spaced homes, the manicured lawns and sculpted hedges. "I told you, I've only been to Midville a couple of times—whatever's on the other side of this neighborhood, I don't know how to get there!"

"Yes. You do," Betty insisted through her teeth. Then, grabbing the wheel, she shoved down on his right leg again, and the four-door jumped the curb with a bone-shaking thud. Wheels skidding, they flew over the sidewalk and tore through the grass, the car bouncing and juddering as they followed the beast at what was definitely an unsafe speed.

The sound that came out of Archie's mouth as they flashed through the narrow side lawn, the mirror on his side crunching and snapping off as they scraped past a carved gatepost, could best be described as a terrified yodel.

Plowing across backyards and between two more houses, they caught sight of the brown wolf again as they barreled back into the moonlight, a dark shape fleeing up the sidewalk on all fours. Archie careened out onto the road again, swerving left, the engine protesting as he put the pedal down. They were on a hill, the street sloping up, and the car inexplicably began to lose speed.

"What's happening?" Betty asked, one arm already out the window as she prepared to haul herself into the open again. "Why are we slowing down? Go faster—we're gonna lose him!"

"I'm trying!" Archie snapped back, stomping his foot on the gas as the wolf reached the crest of the hill . . . but the car didn't respond. The speedometer kept dropping, orange lights blinking to life on the dashboard. "Something's wrong, Betts, I think, uh . . . I think we messed up the gas tank?"

With a string of panicked expletives, Betty hoisted herself up, thrusting her gun over the hood of the car—but she was already too late. The werewolf vanished beyond the peak, while the four-door first coasted to a stop and then started rolling backward. Before Archie even managed to find the brake with his foot, Betty was already scrambling the rest of the way out the window, tumbling onto the street.

"Betts?" he shouted, throwing the gear shift into park. "Betty, what are you doing?" But she was up and off like a shot, racing pell-mell for the point where the beast had disappeared from sight, and Archie had no choice but to rip the keys from the ignition, grab his own weapon, and run after her. "Hey, wait, be careful!"

At the pace the creature moved, there was no way they could hope to keep up with it on foot, let alone overtake it; but that fact didn't slow Betty down at all. Muscles burning, Archie bolted over the rise a few feet behind her, just in time for them to catch sight of the wolf once more—already at the bottom of the hill again, where it took the sharp corner of a T-intersection and vanished behind a thick stand of trees. A moment later, there was a violent *crash-clang* of metal followed by an explosion of breaking glass, and the two teenagers exchanged a startled glance as they chased after the noise.

Reaching the base of the slope, they stumbled to a halt, breathing hard and staring at what rose before them. Past a grandly arched entryway, an imposing building loomed against the sky, a sign out front greeting them in large, colorful letters: WELCOME TO THE MIDVILLE AQUARIUM! The gate that blocked the drive after hours had been smashed open—and it still drifted lazily on its hinges, squeaking faintly as it rebounded from the force necessary to snap its locks.

Archie shot Betty another glance, his neck clammy with sweat, and he arched a brow. "The aquarium?"

Staring at the building's broad, darkened windows, she answered, "I'd make a 'fish in a barrel' joke, but . . . you know. We might turn out to be the fish."

"Do you think there's a security guard around?" He tried not to sound too hopeful.

"I think," Betty said, slipping one more silver bullet into her revolver to replace the one she'd fired from the car, "that you and I are the only security Midville has right now."

With that, she darted forward, slipping through the swinging gate, moonlight painting her blond hair a pale blue. For a moment, Archie was rooted in place, eyes locked on the shining, black windows of the aquarium. It was deserted . . . but not quite deserted enough. If that wolf really was his best friend, then something very bad was going to happen tonight. Either they would have to kill Jughead . . .

Or Jughead would have to kill them.

TWENTY-THREE

THE MIDVILLE AQUARIUM HAD an angular, space-age look to it, with dark cladding and tinted glass that reflected back the stars. Inside, it housed thousands of creatures, from otters and eels to fish from parts of the ocean the sun never reached—and tonight, it seemed, it also housed a werewolf. At the top of the wide front steps, one of the vast windows looking into the foyer had been completely shattered, a gaping hole giving them a clear view of the black void within.

Most of the Riverdale kids had been to the aquarium at least once before, either on a field trip or with their families, but Betty's last visit had been in fifth grade. She remembered almost nothing of the layout inside and didn't know what kind of situation they were heading into. Holding the revolver steady in a two-handed grip, broken glass crunching under her feet, she sidled through the damaged window and into the building.

The foyer was vast and sleek, with heavy shadows pouring down from a high ceiling, and as far as either of them could tell it was empty. There were some plants and benches, a shuttered gift shop, and a circular reception desk backed by a wall-mounted floor plan, but no monsters in sight. The aquarium was a loop, Betty realized, with the entrance to the exhibits on the left of the entrance hall, and the exit facing it from the opposite side.

"Where is he?" Archie whispered the question, his voice still bouncing conspicuously off the marble floor and polished stone walls. A thousand bits of tinted glass were scattered over the ground, but there was no indication of which direction the wolf had gone, and a clock above the door ticked forebodingly as Betty stared at the blueprint on the wall.

"We'll have to split up," she finally said, wishing there was a better answer. "It's the only way we can make sure he doesn't escape. You go that way, I'll go the other, and we cut off his way out. He'll be cornered between us."

"Right. He'll be cornered." Archie looked queasy, but he nodded as he followed the direction of her pointed finger— to the darkened arch on the far side of the foyer that marked the exit from the tour of displays.

He started walking, slowly and deliberately, the dragging steps of a condemned man, and Betty called after him. "If you see the wolf . . . you have to shoot, Archie. No matter who it is. If you hesitate, even for a second, it'll be too late. For both of us."

"Yeah. Yeah, I get it." He forced a smile that didn't meet his eyes, holding up the handgun. "'Kill to be kind.'"

And then he was gone, eaten by the shadows, and Betty turned to face her own dark path. The start of the aquarium's exhibits was a narrow, zigzag hallway bordered by informational plaques showing a timeline of aquatic life across the eons. Its recessed lights turned off for the night, the only illumination available was a creepy blue-green glow filtering in from the passageway's far end. Betty swallowed hard as she inched along, adjusting her sweaty grip on the revolver, trying not to think about all the ways this might be a huge mistake.

She'd been a fool not to take it for granted from the start that they were dealing with more than one wolf. It was rare these days, but obviously not unheard of, and the fact of it threw certain past events into sharp focus, such as Dilton's death inside an old crypt and the locked-room mystery of Miss Grundy's tragic end. These situations had the authorities thoroughly perplexed, but to Betty they finally made sense. Two wolves working together—one to set a trap, the other to guide their prey into it—explained the unexplainable.

And now she and Archie had followed a werewolf into a scenario where they had to split up, creeping through nearly pitch-black corridors with nowhere to run and nowhere to hide. Every inch of her skin pebbled with goose bumps as she was forced to consider that the beast was not the one who was about to be cornered in the aquarium.

The narrow hallway opened onto a square room lined with different-sized fish tanks, the water inside shimmering turquoise under soft, hidden bulbs. Tetras, guppies, and barbs dove and circled, casting a net of shapeless, undulating shadows across every surface in the room, and Betty glanced around nervously. Everything was silent but for the whir of filtration systems and the occasional rush of bubbles breaking, and she squeezed her eyes shut for just a second before creeping ahead to the next doorway.

Two more rooms followed that looked no different, wallpapered with mirages conjured by light through rippling water, and the muscles in her jaw started to ache from tension. On the opposite side of the aquarium, Archie would be going through something just like this, trying to keep his head clear as he closed in on a monster that had no way out—except over one of their dead bodies. She hoped he wouldn't be the one to find the wolf, because she wasn't sure he'd put himself first.

Then again, she was starting to wonder if *she* would.

The third room opened onto a long, curving passage bordered on both sides by massive tanks of dark blue water. One contained a school of translucent jellyfish, their motions mesmerizing, tentacles streaming like ribbons from their bell-shaped heads; and the other held a brightly colored universe of angelfish. This was what Betty remembered best from her one and only visit—these triangular bodies, with dramatic fins and brilliant scales, darting back and forth in a seamless, chaotic ballet. She'd watched them for what had felt like hours. Seeing them now, she let out a sigh that echoed along the glass-enclosed corridor, a breath that contained multitudes.

A breath that was answered.

It came from the far end of the hallway, a huff of air so faint it was almost drowned out by the growing thud of her heartbeat; but the sound was unmistakable—and inhuman. Pivoting slowly, her hackles rising, Betty took one cautious step along the slight bend in the passage . . . and froze. Two glowing eyes, narrowed into menacing slits, glared back at her; two long, pointed ears folded back against a lupine head in a threatening signal; and four massive paws, the size of human hands, scraped the tiled floor.

From its muzzle to the tip of its tail, each hair of the were-wolf's thick brown pelt quivered with deadly energy as it took one menacing step forward.

Betty had the revolver up and sighted, the barrel trained on the spot between the beast's eyes, in the time it took her to blink. Choking on the first breath she drew, she braced herself, steadying her hand—and wondered why she hadn't pulled the trigger yet.

Or maybe not wondering. She could still feel Ethel's paws pinning her shoulders to that mountain of trash; she could still remember the taste and smell of blood spraying across her face; she could still see that severed wolf's head slowly reverting back to its human shape, familiar eyes staring emptily and accusingly back at her. No matter how many hours she'd spent training, no matter how many missions she'd gone on with her parents or Aunt Elena, nothing had prepared her for that last moment. For killing someone she knew.

If she pulled the trigger right now, would the beast in front of her turn into Jughead Jones as it died? The barrel of the gun wavered slightly, a bead of perspiration rolling down her temple, and she took another shaky breath. *"Sometimes you have to kill to be kind."* Growling deeper in its throat, the creature bared even more of its teeth, quivering all over—and Betty blinked in surprise.

It was scared. The flatted ears, the raised fur, the

trembling . . . the beast was frightened of her. The revolver dipped, her head spinning with the realization.

And that's when the werewolf finally lunged.

👑👑👑

He was staring at a betta fish, its extravagant pink tail fluttering in slow motion, when the roar of gunfire sent Archie's heart catapulting so far up his throat he almost gagged on it. The report was muffled, coming from far away, but the sound was unmistakable. Archie's vision tunneled, his head growing light.

Betty.

Breaking into a run, he sprinted through three more rooms, barely thinking to check his surroundings before plunging ahead into the next stretch of unknown territory. His hands were sweaty, and terror squeezed his chest tight as he thought about Betty and the wolf. He'd been so sure that he would be the one to find the beast first, that his luck was just that lousy. He'd been so sure that Betty would be the only living thing in the entire aquarium to walk out alive at the end of the night.

There'd only been one gunshot. That meant either Betty had stopped the beast . . . or that it had stopped her. Nausea swept over him, and dark spots crowded his vision, his feet stumbling as he swayed against the wall. In his hand, the gun shook so badly he could barely hold it.

Whose body was he running to?

Which of his friends was dead?

Forcing himself to keep moving, he staggered down a short hallway and into a cavernous room at the rear of the aquarium, where an entire wall of thick glass held back the largest tank of water Archie had ever seen. Rocks and shells covered its floor, dark plant life poking through and waving softly—and above, high over his head, two distinctive figures circled. Casting shadows that slithered across the floor at his feet, silhouetted by oblique light, a pair of hammerhead sharks drifted in ominous silence.

The weird light from the tank rippled and danced over the room's concrete floor, the resonance of electricity humming faintly in the air . . . and then the sound of a deep, frightening growl rumbled out from the black archway leading off into the next section of the loop. Archie froze all the way to his core as two burning yellow eyes appeared in the shadows, and a massive brown wolf prowled soundlessly out of the passage and into the light.

"J-Jughead?" His voice squeaked, sweat rolling down his sternum. The wolf came to a stop, snarling as it pulled its ears back flat against its skull, and all the moisture left Archie's mouth. "Jug, is . . . is that you, man?"

Snapping its jaws at the air, the werewolf bared all its teeth, a sling of drool spilling to the floor. Archie's bladder weakened dangerously, and he took an instinctive step back. With a quaking hand, he aimed the weapon, lowered it . . . and then aimed it again, his nausea returning with the force of a tidal wave.

"Jug, if you're in there, you gotta listen to me," he begged, barely getting any sound out through his sandpaper throat. The beast crept to the left, claws ticking against the floor, and Archie moved quickly to the right, keeping the gun up between them. "I don't want to shoot you, okay? I don't want anyone else to get hurt, and I know you don't, either—that's why you chained yourself up tonight. You can fight this, man, I know you can!"

It was a great speech that would all turn out to be wasted air if the thing in front of him was actually Bingo—especially if he'd already killed Betty. But he had to try. He had to believe. Peering into the creature's eyes, he struggled to see past its terrifying features, past that unearthly glow. Minutely, the beast cocked its head, the feral expression changing . . . and Archie drew a breath. For just a moment, less than a heartbeat, he'd seen something in the shape of its face that he recognized. Something he *knew*.

"That *is* you, isn't it?" He gaped, his heart pounding in his ears. The creature in front of him was Jughead, he was sure of it. The beast stepped back with a confused whine, snapping at the air again, and then prowled back to the right before baring its teeth once more. Holding up a hand beside the gun, Archie backed away a little. "Whoa, whoa, whoa, come on, Jug! It's me—Archie. Your best friend? Remember?"

The wolf hesitated and then whined again, making a confused noise that vibrated through the air. Shaking its head, dark fur rippling from the point of its muzzle all the way down to its flanks, the beast paced back and forth a little and then snarled again.

"That's it, man, keep fighting," Archie pleaded. "Don't give in to this. I know you're not a killer, and . . . and neither am I." Adrenaline spitting ice-cold nails through his bloodstream, he lowered his gun to the floor, hoping it wasn't the worst—and last—mistake he'd ever make. "I'm not going to hurt you, Jug. That's not who we are, and it's not who we have to be. Whatever caused this, I know you didn't ask for it. I know you don't want to be a monster, but you have to fight it, man!"

"You have to fight it, man." A part of Jughead's buried consciousness made sense of those words and shouted the meaning at him through a thick screen of intrinsic, animal instinct—some tiny voice telling him to stop, to listen. But it was hard to hear over the grinding rumble of his empty

stomach. The intoxicating scent of fear hung heavy in the air; he was hungry for it, and all of his being demanded that he *attack*.

Drawing back, Jughead calculated the distance between him and his prey, assessing how much force he'd have to put behind a leap; and then that voice intruded again, a shrill alarm warning him not to proceed. He recognized Archie, of course—just as he'd recognized Dilton and Grundy and Pop Tate—but he couldn't understand his own hesitation. Knowing who you were hunting was an *advantage*; what was keeping him from seizing it?

Jughead paced, shaking his head in an unstrung silence. His body quivered with the need to pounce, and the confusion of not being able to follow through on the impulse frightened him. A frustrated whine emerged from deep in his gut, and he drew back again, teeth snapping, summoning up the clarity of his primal urge to kill. He was just about to force himself to lunge when a new scent caught his attention—and he knew, instantly, that they weren't alone in the room anymore . . .

♛♛♛

Maybe putting the gun down had been a stupid idea, but it was too late now. The wolf took a step forward, and then two steps back, and made a pitiful crooning noise. Then it narrowed its eyes and gnashed its teeth, coiling back like it was about to spring, and Archie's head whirled in fear. But before it could pounce, another dark shape separated unexpectedly from the shadowy corridor leading away to the rest of the loop, pale light from the shark tank gleaming against blond hair and the shining barrel of a revolver.

"Archie, don't move," Betty commanded, her tone crisp and clear, her weapon held steady on the werewolf. She didn't appear injured, but she was soaking wet, water dripping from her bedraggled ponytail. "I don't want to shoot you by accident."

The beast growled, its attention caught by Betty's unexpected entrance, and it shifted its feet warily. Looking from one human to the other, it seemed to be sizing up the threat they posed, and its ears pulled back even farther as the scruff on its neck lifted. Licking his lips, Archie pleaded, "Wait, Betty! This is . . . it's Jughead. It's Jughead in there."

"I'm sorry, Archie." Betty could have been a statue for how remote her expression was, but her tone was soft and clear in the empty room. "It doesn't matter. It *can't* matter."

"He's resisting it, Betts, I swear! How can that not matter?" Archie had his eyes on the wolf, on Jughead, whose lips quivered around a deadly array of long, sharp teeth. "He could have killed me already, but he hasn't. Give him a chance!"

"We've both seen what werewolves do when they're given chances," she said, her voice ringing against the shark tank, the lazy shapes inside still circling. But she hadn't pulled the trigger yet. She could have killed already, too—but she hadn't. "We . . . we don't have a choice."

Caught between them, the beast's eyes rolled, its primal fear of being surrounded pushing it further from reason. Holding out both hands, sensing his opportunity slipping away, Archie whimpered, "Please, Jug. I know you can beat this. I believe in you, man."

♔♔♔

"I believe in you, man." This time, the words barely registered. There were two of them now, and Jughead was trapped in the middle, both of the exits blocked. His heart raced, his muscles were tense and tingling, and he dug his paws into the floor. Fear was quickly clouding all his other senses, and he growled louder. Bingo had taught him how to hold back from a kill—how to resist the overwhelming urge to strike until the moment was just right; but no training could overcome the instinct for survival.

He was cornered, and he needed to escape. Everything else—his hunger, his caution, the small voice telling him to stand down—vanished in a haze of fear, replaced by a sense of fight-or-flight that could not be reasoned with. Betty stood on one side, and Archie on the other . . . but only one of them was armed.

His body shook, and one last growl rattled the depths of his gullet . . .

The werewolf trembled all over, a growl seeming to shake its entire body—and then it sprang without warning. Eyes blazing, jaws spreading to catch the air, it launched itself right at Archie. The boy shrank back, nowhere to hide and no weapon to defend himself, his life flashing before his eyes. He barely caught the gleam of gunmetal as Betty's revolver snapped up.

The roar of the gun was shocking, earsplitting, and his heart spiraled all the way up into his brain. His knees gave out a second before the colossal beast crashed into him, and their bodies hit the ground, rolling and skidding over the hard floor. The werewolf's claws ripped open the leather sleeves of Archie's jacket as it tumbled away—finally coming to a stop sprawled on its side, slack and motionless.

Archie struggled up onto his knees just as Betty reached him, her face bloodless, the revolver smoking in her white-knuckled grip. Before them, a pool of blood slowly widened beneath the wolf, as its body gradually shifted back to reveal the limp human form of Jughead Jones.

PART THREE: NEW MOON

THREE WEEKS LATER

EPILOGUE

NOW THAT THE PLACE WAS under new management, the burgers that the Chock'Lit Shoppe served just weren't as good as they used to be. Regardless, Archie and his friends were seated at their usual booth a few days after the grand reopening. The necessary cleanup and renovations had taken a while to complete, and despite aggressive advertising, the diner was nearly empty.

"Well, what did you expect, Archie?" Betty asked under her breath when the boy made note of the sparsely populated tables. "I mean, a man *died*, like, right where we're sitting, for Pete's sake."

Archie couldn't help shuddering a little at the thought, even though there was only one person who really knew exactly where Pop Tate had died—and he wasn't telling anyone the details. Methodically stuffing his face with a pile of

French fries, he was also the one who'd insisted that they come in the first place, and the only person of the three at the table who hadn't complained about the food yet.

"Why are we here, anyway, Jughead?" Archie asked, looking down at his half-eaten burger with a suddenly queasy eye, wondering just how thorough the cleanup job had been. "Isn't it sort of, uh . . . morbid?"

Sitting across from him and Betty, Archie's best friend merely shrugged. "I think I probably owe them the business, since I'm the reason everyone else is staying away. Honestly, they did a great job in here, though. You wouldn't believe how much blood there was."

"Right." Archie swallowed a little and then pushed the rest of his burger aside. He was probably done eating—forever. Lifting up his milk shake instead, he cleared his throat. "Since the three of us are together again at the Chock'Lit Shoppe for the first time since all this started, I would like to propose a toast. Here's to Betty for shooting Jughead in the hip!"

"*Archie,*" Betty admonished, her cheeks turning pink.

Jughead didn't seem the least bit perturbed, though. Lifting his shake, he said, "Thank you for shooting me, Betty."

"Any time." She rolled her eyes, but allowed the boys to click the edges of their cups against her own. That night at the aquarium, when Jughead's instincts had prevailed at last and he'd leaped straight for Archie's throat, it was only Betty's quick reflexes and deadeye aim that had saved both boys' lives.

The first shot she'd fired that night, in the long corridor by the jellyfish tank, had been reactive and unplanned. Thankfully, it had scared Jughead away, but it had also struck one of the thick glass panes on the wall; cracks had spread in a matter of seconds, and then a deluge of salt water and gelatinous blobs with stinging tentacles had poured out. Thank God the creatures weren't deadly. When she'd recovered, she'd managed to make her way to the hammerhead room just in time.

From her position, with the light from the tank, she'd had a clear kill shot . . . but she hadn't taken it. Instead, she'd put a round into one of Jughead's haunches, the silver bullet lodging high up in his femur, its poison gradually forcing his body to reverse the change.

Together, she and Archie had barely managed to carry Jughead out of the aquarium, "borrow" a car off the road, and get the boy back to Elena's gym before he bled out. Once there, they'd removed the bullet and then locked the unconscious werewolf up in Cousin Jacob's empty cage while his supernatural healing took over. Thanks to some Cooper family connections, they'd even managed to get both the

Beetle and Archie's four-door towed to safety before either vehicle could be identified and linked to a crime scene.

"Seriously, Betty," Jughead mumbled, staring into his milk shake. "Thanks. You gave me a chance, even though you didn't have to. Even though I . . . I did some really awful stuff."

"That wasn't your fault." Archie's response was immediate, but Jughead waved off the excuse.

"I didn't ask to be the way I am, but I'm the only one there is to blame for what happened to Pop Tate," Jughead said solemnly—and Archie squirmed once again. Was he *really* not going to tell them where he ate the man? Giving both his friends a meek smile, Jughead added, "Whether I like it or not, I'm a monster. And you guys didn't have to save my life."

"You earned a chance, Juggie." Betty was firm, interrupting Archie before he could argue against Jughead some more. "I've . . . in all the time I've spent studying and hunting werewolves, I've never seen what I saw that night. Even when you were completely transformed, you still fought the urge to kill." Poking her straw up and down in her milk shake, she admitted, "My cousin spent his whole life learning to think of lycanthropes as the enemy—learning to beat them any way he could. But when it happened to him, he still wasn't strong enough to do what you did."

"And now, thanks to the power of wolfsbane, you're even stronger!" Archie couldn't keep the smugness out of his voice, and Betty rolled her eyes again.

"Yeah, yeah. Cheers to Archie." Her tone was dry, but she lifted her milk shake anyway, and they all toasted. Despite her many doubts and ominous predictions, at Archie's insistence, she'd gotten Jughead a supply of wolfsbane. For the next two nights, they'd dosed him and then locked him in the cage—and on both occasions, he'd shifted only briefly from his human form before turning back. It was frankly pretty remarkable. He wasn't "cured," of course, and he still had to be confined for safety's sake, but it was another thing Betty had never seen before. "I honestly didn't think it would work, but you proved me wrong, Juggie."

"To be fair, your family's whole 'shoot first, ask questions never' approach to werewolves probably limits the number of successful experiments," Jughead replied bluntly. There was an awkward silence that he did not seem the least bit aware of, and then he asked, "Does your aunt still hate me?"

"Elena doesn't *hate* you; she just thinks you should be dead." Betty was equally blunt. Convincing her aunt to let Jughead take up residency in the empty cage had been difficult, to say the least, and many strong words about "sacred duty" and "walking, bloodthirsty nightmares" had been exchanged. "But it's not her call. The mission was mine, and this is how I'm handling it. For now."

Jughead was still learning to control his condition, to resist his violent instincts while under the thrall of the full moon, and if he ever slipped up . . . well, it wasn't something any of them wanted to think about too much.

"Is there any word on Jacob?" Archie asked, trying to head off another awkward silence.

"According to Elena, it looks like he may have fled the country." Betty shook her head. "She's going down to Mexico next week to follow up on a lead. There's another family of longtime hunters down there who have offered her backup if she needs it."

"And have you heard anything about . . . you know, the investigation?" Jughead wouldn't look either of them in the eye.

"According to Kevin Keller, his dad says the case is in sort of a holding pattern. All the evidence points to animal attacks, but aside from a couple of very tenuous reports from terrified residents in a certain Midville neighborhood, no one has reported any sightings that match the kind of creature that could be responsible." Betty set her milk shake aside, clearing her throat. "Because of the established pattern, they're expecting more deaths next week when the full moon returns, but they don't have any leads to pursue right now." Glancing up at Jughead, she added, "Officially, Ethel Muggs and Bingo Wilkin have been named the last known victims of the Riverdale Ripper."

That awkward silence returned to the table, and they shared a round of dark, meaningful glances. Because the crime scene where Ethel's body had been found was covered in animal hair and surrounded by massive paw prints, the conclusion that she had fallen prey to the Ripper had been easy to jump to. Bingo's case, however, was a little less cut-and-dried.

The Wilkin home had been utterly destroyed, with not much left but the severely water-damaged basement, once the fire department was done putting out the blaze. Lying among the structure's charred remnants, however, investigators had found a severed limb—an arm, the shoulder joint exhibiting the deep scoring of bite marks. DNA testing had proved that the body part belonged to Bingo, who had been missing since the night the house exploded . . . but no other remains had been found, human or animal.

"Maybe he just, you know . . . *kablow*," Archie suggested, not for the first time, making a motion with his hand as if to suggest Bingo's body going completely up in smoke. "Jug said he was in the kitchen, right next to the gas main when the blast happened . . . maybe it was so hot and intense he just, like, disintegrated."

"And maybe he was blown out the back door." Jughead fidgeted nervously with his hat, tilting it first one way and then the other. It was a new hat, to replace the one that had been destroyed in the inferno—and even though it was identical to his old one, he still swore it didn't fit the same.

"So what if he was?" Archie's hands felt unsteady, and he took a gulp of milk shake that went down as thick and slimy as an oyster. "We saw the house go 'boom,' remember? It was a total fireball. Even if he got thrown clear by the blast, he was probably a charcoal briquette by the time he landed in the backyard."

"Werewolves heal really fast," Jughead pointed out. "Didn't you tell me Betty said there were stories of them regenerating whole limbs? Like, for example, *missing arms?*"

Archie turned to the blond girl beside him. "Betts, have you ever heard of a charcoal briquette spontaneously poofing back into a werewolf after getting blown out of an exploding house?"

"I'm just saying." Jughead's voice was tiny, his eyes fixed on his fingernails. "He might . . . he could still be out there. Right?"

"Maybe he is, and maybe he isn't," Betty finally stated after an interminable pause. Then she turned and looked through the broad windows of the diner, gazing up at the gathering twilight and the waxing gibbous moon slowly rising in the evening sky. "I guess we've got about seven days until we know for sure."

Jughead peered even closer at his fingernails, blurting, "I want to help you track him down. If . . . if he's really alive, I mean."

Snapping her eyes back from the window, Betty blinked. "Juggie—"

"After everything that happened, after everything I—we— did . . . I have to do whatever I can to make sure he won't hurt anyone else." Jughead finally met her gaze, his expression meek. "Please?"

"I . . . I don't know, Juggie." Betty shifted uncomfortably, turning over her hand in a one-armed shrug. "You've got a lot to deal with already; right now you need to be focused on controlling your shifts as much as you can."

"But that's just it." He gave her a smart look. "I know how he thinks, both as a human and a wolf—and he's my pack, remember? When I change, I'll be compelled to seek him out anyway."

"It's not like we can put a leash on you," Betty pointed out, making a face. "And it is kind of too soon to have this conversation. For all we know, Bingo really *is* a charcoal briquette."

"*Thank* you." Archie spread his hands out.

"I can help with other things, too, though." Jughead

remained as stubborn as ever. "I'm only a monster three days a month, but the rest of the time I can do research and make phone calls and stuff." Snatching a napkin from the metal box on the table, he added, "Anyway, it's not just about Bingo. I've got a lot to make up for, and if other werewolves turn up, I want to help stop them, too. I owe it to the people I killed, I owe it to you guys for giving me a chance, and . . . and I owe it to Ethel."

Betty went silent again—which wasn't unusual these days, when Ethel's name came up; but something in the tightness of her expression, in the way her finger traced a nervous pattern in the sweat on her water glass, made Archie's hackles rise. "Betts? Is, uh . . . is something wrong?"

She took a deep breath, and her shoulders slumped. "Ethel Muggs. For three whole weeks, I've been trying to make sense of what happened to her."

"Betty, you need to let go of the guilt." Archie was firm. He'd been reading up on this, so he'd know exactly what to say when the subject arose. "You're not the one who made her a monster, and it was self-def—"

"That's not what I mean," she cut him off with a faint smile, "but thank you. What I don't understand is why Bingo *bit* her."

"It was probably an accident." Jughead frowned. "They were making out, his teeth slipped, and . . . oopsy?"

"Maybe." Betty didn't look convinced. "Bingo made out with lots of girls, though. He had . . . experience. Ethel made it sound like he was *chewing* on her—like it was deliberate."

"Maybe he wanted to create confusion?" Archie's scalp prickled, a brilliant deduction blossoming. "Bodies were piling up, people were starting to panic . . . he had to figure that sooner or later a hunter would get involved."

"Or the FBI," Jughead interjected thoughtfully. "The sheriff's department doesn't have a huge budget, and if they attributed the deaths to a serial killer or something they'd be able to bring in outside help."

Archie nodded. "If Ethel got all hairy and went bananas in public, everyone would think *she* was the Riverdale Ripper all along."

"And because she wouldn't have known what was happening to her, or how to deal with it, there was a better chance of someone tracking her and killing her, letting Bingo off the hook . . ." Betty pursed her lips. "That's possible."

"Or maybe," Jughead began, after a moment, "he did it because he was a cruel, malignant sociopath who liked making people suffer." His voice was quiet and chilling. "Maybe the only thing he wanted to create was chaos and terror—because he thought it was fun."

"That's the one that's got me worried." Betty toyed with her fork, pressing her thumb against the tines as a rueful smile twisted her mouth. "Because what if . . . what if Bingo bit other girls, too? What if Riverdale is filled with ticking, were-wolf time bombs, just waiting to go off?" She turned back to the windows. "What if Bingo still being out there is only the least of our worries?"

A long silence fell over the table, until Archie cleared his throat. "Then we've got a week to investigate—and to be ready, no matter what."

For a long time, they stayed at their booth in the Chock'Lit Shoppe, watching stars poke through the dark-ness outside—and making plans.

ABOUT THE AUTHOR

Caleb Roehrig is an author of young adult thrillers, including *Last Seen Leaving*, *White Rabbit*, and *Death Prefers Blondes*. A native of Ann Arbor, Michigan, he has also lived in Chicago, Los Angeles, and Helsinki, Finland. As a former actor and television producer, Roehrig has experience on both sides of the camera, with a résumé that includes appearances on film and TV—not to mention seven years in the stranger-than-fiction salt mines of reality television. In the name of earning a paycheck, he has: hung around a frozen cornfield in his underwear, partied with an actual rock star, chatted with a scandal-plagued politician, and been menaced by a disgruntled ostrich.